Jamaican Backyard

Memories and Musings

Jamaican Backyard

Memories and Musings

By
Ronald E. Glegg

Jamaican Backyard
Published through Lulu.com

Book Design and Layout by
www.integrativeink.com

TABLE OF CONTENTS

BLUE MOUNTAIN DREAM

The mountain looms like a blue giant, one mile tall, standing in the middle of the island. Clouds rush past the giant's head, driven by the steady northeast trade winds. A narrow, steep, mossy trail winds like a helix up and around the body of the giant. A goat and a mongoose guard the entrance to the trail. I bow to each of the two sentries and deliver my password. They consult in whispers, then signal me to go forward. I struggle upwards, breathing deeply in the warm air.

A pure blue stream of water gushes out of the red earth and falls away over a cliff to unseen depths; I dare not look down. I cup my hands and drink the cool liquid; it has the flavor of honey. Maidenhair ferns grow in delicate clumps along the banks of the stream, thriving in the shade and the damp earth, waving dainty, green leaves in the mountain breeze. Banana trees grow on each side of the trail and drape their fronds to form a tunnel of green umbrellas. Not to be outdone, bamboo trees send up supple, curving branches to construct arches for a gothic cathedral. The smooth, tight skins of red coffee beans glisten like rubies even in the subdued light. Heliconias brighten the forest with dazzling red and yellow blooms.

A handsome lizard with green stripes and spots of yellow, blue and brown moves in short dashes, jerks its head from side to side, as if to take in all the scenery. It leaves footprints on the moss. Hummingbirds dart from flower to flower and search for nectar with their needle-like beaks. Giant butterflies cluster in groups and flutter through the branches while bees are busy building honeycombs.

Suddenly, near the top of the mountain, I come upon a garden hidden away in a quiet corner, surrounded by a rainbow made of hibiscus and oleander bushes in full bloom. The strong aroma of jasmine, mint, and thyme hang heavily around me. The garden seems like a place where all plants, animals, and humans could live together in harmony, without anger, evil, hate, or fear, a place where love would thrive. I rest there.

A clip-clop breaks through the tranquil forest. A donkey appears around the corner, followed by a woman and two small angels who skip along at her side; one cherub white; and the other black. A crown of red bougainvillea and yellow mountain lilies adorns the donkey's head. The woman wears a green and black bandanna on her head, a gold band around one ankle, and her feet are bare. Brown, wavy hair interwoven with silver threads reaches all the way down her back. Mangos, oranges, and avocados fill the two straw hampers that hang from the donkey's back.

The group moves down the trail towards me. I step aside to give them clear passage. As they pass by, the woman comes close and utters a cheerful greeting.

"Welcome to Paradise!" She stops for a moment and smiles at me. I start to reply, but no sound comes out of my mouth. I reach out to touch her face, but my hand seems not long enough. At that moment, as I try to speak to the woman, a thick, black cloud floats over the giant and shuts out the light. It is dark; I feel cold and apprehensive. The children, the woman, and the donkey fade from view. I am alone again.

JAMAICAN BACKYARD

The solid concrete fence that enclosed our yard was eight feet high, crowned with sharp, jagged pieces of green, broken glass embedded in the cement. My father and mother designed the mini-fortress to keep their five children safely in, to guarantee privacy from the house next door, and to keep out prowlers and thieves. Everything happened in the backyard of our home, where I lived from the day of my birth until I was twenty years old.

In contrast with the lawn and rose garden in the front of the house, not one blade of grass survived in the backyard, because of the constant everyday activities that compacted the soil and left the surface with a thin coating of fine dust.

Six mango trees rose forty feet or more, providing partial shade from the searing heat of the merciless tropical sun. There was always a shady place to sit, play, or misbehave. Sometimes, when gusty winds shook the tree limbs, the golden-red, peach-like mangos fell to the ground. The riper fruits broke open from the impact, and yellow juice ran on the brown earth to form sticky puddles. The challenge was to catch a mango in midair; the reward was to overeat on the aromatic, fleshy, most delicious fruit in the world.

A lignum vitae tree displayed its leathery leaves and azure flowers. It was difficult to cut into the hard, dense "wood of life" to carve a name or a date; but the shallowest bruise oozed a sticky liquid resembling honey; this gradually hardened into round, transparent balls of gum that looked like precious amber. At dusk, chickens scrambled into the tree to roost for the night. At dawn, they crowed and cackled, flopped rather than flew down, and made painful thuds as their plump little bodies hit the ground and sent feathers flying all around.

The chickens represented only part of the mini-zoo in the yard. Outdoor cages housed canaries, parrots, and multicolored lovebirds. Together they sang bird-operas all day and into the night. Pigeons cooed, strutted, cuddled up to each other, and collected food for their ravenous, half-naked squabs. Ducks found secret places under the house to lay their eggs, and then sat on them patiently for weeks until they hatched. The fluffy, golden baby ducks that we called "dillies" paraded single file, back and forth across the yard behind their proud, protective mothers. Their webbed feet left fan-shaped imprints in the dust.

Two mongrel dogs that could digest anything, even fish bones, roamed around, sniffed, and molested the other animals, especially unprotected chicks as well as squabs that had fallen from their nests.

Foot-long green lizards scurried so fast that they made a rustling sound on the earth. Sometimes they sat still like statues, flaps of yellow skin hanging down beneath their necks; the yellow decoy attracted flies to be caught with one fast flip of a tongue.

A pet turtle crawled around aimlessly, as if it suffered from amnesia, moving its wrinkled head in and out of the shell house. Guinea pigs and rabbits coexisted in the same cage, and chomped incessantly on succulent grass and scraps of leftover vegetables.

Clotheslines stretched from tree to tree. The odor of burning wood signaled washday; water in a metal tub boiled on the fire. Victoria, the washerwoman, dripped with sweat from her strenuous efforts to scrub, rinse, squeeze, and wring each piece of clothing by hand. When the soggy laundry was hung out to dry, water evaporated quickly in the warm breeze and the refreshing smell of clean cloth drifted through the air.

I cannot believe that I sometimes threw dust on the wet cloths just because I was angry about something, such as having been punished. The clothes had to be washed again, and I had to be punished again.

A dozen or more children from the neighborhood came often to play games in our backyard--soccer, cricket, baseball, marbles, and fighting. Balls flew in all directions, endangering the smaller animals, and occasionally breaking windows.

How was it possible that so many large trees could have grown in the limited space of our small backyard? Each tree in the world has a special significance, a unique existence, and plays its own role. Some trees spread their branches like umbrellas to provide shade, while others display the beauty of their leaves, flowers, and bark. Some are perfect for birds to nest in, termites to bore into, horses to rub against, and for dogs to leave messages on. For children, trees were created for climbing, for hanging swings and ropes attached to old rubber tires, and for carving dates and the names of secret loves.

The mango trees in our backyard fulfilled nearly all the requirements of a universal tree. The limbs were sturdy, strong, and flexible. The lower ones grew close enough to the ground so that with little effort, I could climb up the rough trunk and into the tree. The branches and limbs were spaced perfectly for me to move around and pretend to be Tarzan or his chimpanzee, Cheetah.

On a windy day, when the northeast trade winds blew at full speed, the whole tree gyrated in perpetual motion as it pitched and rolled. I remember the exhilarating feeling, perched forty feet above the earth, of swaying back and forth, up and down. I wished I were a bird. The limbs creaked and that sound added an element of excitement, danger, and fear. Sometimes I regretted climbing into the tree, but then fear would be displaced by the challenge and beauty of what I could see. From the top of the oscillating tree, I would look beyond the narrow plain that rimmed the little island, across the endless expanse of the aquamarine Caribbean Sea, and out to the horizon. The unpolluted air was crystal clear in those days. The horizon was a distinct line drawn with indigo. I would hold on for dear life, certain that I had climbed to the highest point in the world. But why couldn't I see anything else, no other part of the world?

I would gaze and stare into the far distance. Gradually, a piece of land would appear above the dark line of the horizon. First, it was a shapeless blur, and then an outline appeared and disappeared. I pretended it was Cuba. The vision was real but not real, a mere phantom, a mirage, and a dream world. If only I could travel to Havana.

A red-winged black bird would whistle from a branch nearby, feathers ruffled by the wind, little black claws wrapped securely around the smallest branch, an insect held in its beak. The head moved in jerky, furtive motions as the cautious bird looked all around, then flew away to feed its fledglings in a nest somewhere, leaving me stranded in my tree.

The vultures known as John crows circled far above the treetop, keeping me company. These black, whirling birds stood out in bold contrast against a sky that seemed at times more white than blue because of the intense, blinding sunlight. When seen up close on the ground, these scrawny creatures are awkward and unattractive. They could win an ugly contest for birds. Heads and necks are bald, revealing bare, wrinkled, blood red skin. Their dull feathers do not lie flat and tidy like those of other birds, but stick out as if they needed to be brushed or combed into place. The beaks and claws are designed and built to rip and tear apart dead animals. Few birds in the world fly with the ease, grace, and confidence of John crows. They glide, float, soar, and circle endlessly, looking for a meal. Carried by the wind, they ride on currents of air, playing in the updrafts. Sometimes they appear to be as stationary as a kite in a steady wind, seldom condescending to flap their fully extended wings. Their majestic, synchronized aerial ballets combine hypnotically with the movement of the tree, suspending me above earth and reality. The birds and I used free tickets to freedom.

It is harder to climb down a tree than up it. Going up, you can see each branch and plan exactly where to place your feet and grasp with your hands. But climbing down, you see only your hands in front and above you, and need to guess and feel with your feet.

Climb trees often enough and you will eventually slip and fall. It happened to me when I was nine years old. It was an annatto tree. I climbed up to pick the spiny capsules, then rolled off a limb about four feet above the ground and landed on my head. Blood ran through my hair, down my face, all over my clothes. My bawling must have been loud enough to reach the entire neighborhood. Many people ran to my rescue. I thought I was sure to die.

Having been told by phone about the accident, my father left his workplace and arrived soon after, riding in his own horse and buggy. I visited the Kingston General Hospital as a patient for the first time. The sight of all the busy white uniforms made me feel very important. But at the same time I wondered who washed the uniforms.

Someone poured iodine on the wound, since that was the most widely used disinfectant in those days. The burning sensation hurt more than the pain in my head. The doctor closed the scalp wound with several stitches. The white scar is one inch long. No hair grows on that relic from my days of climbing trees. The tree disappeared that same day. My father cut it down. I have no way of knowing whether he was motivated by anger, fear, or love. But I think he was just carried away by the moment and took it out on the tree.

Along one side of the backyard, a rectangular building about fifty feet long was located approximately twenty feet from our house. It was covered with a corrugated zinc roof and partitioned into five rooms. One room had been set aside for washing clothes and for bathing in a concrete tub about six feet long and three feet high. By virtue of its age and continuous use, the concrete had turned green and smooth, like polished marble. Before climbing over the edge and into the bath, early-morning bathers had best check for five-inch-long, brown scorpions, armed with stings in their curved tails. They might have crawled or fallen into the bath overnight.

A kitchen was adjacent to the bathroom, then a bedroom for the cook, followed by a room in which to iron clothes and store odds and ends. The toilet, with two holes in a wooden bench, was mercifully segregated at the far end, away from the house. Each of the windowless rooms had only one door, which faced on the backyard.

Animals, birds, insects, and children flourished in these colorful surroundings. All creatures were welcome.

From day to day, everybody who had something to sell or a service to provide stopped in our backyard. Some vendors announced themselves from a distance with bells and ear-piercing street cries. The fish lady screamed the same words over and over in a high-pitched, falsetto voice:

"Feesh! Feesh! Fre-esh Feesh!"

She arrived wearing a bright, multicolored, plaid bandanna wrapped around her head, and a loose-fitting skirt made from the same cotton fabric as her headdress. On top of her head, she balanced a brown, handmade basket, bleached and discolored by

7

the sun. A bundle of cloth served as a soft cushion between her head and the old basket. She walked with a graceful swaying of hips and body; her strong, muscular neck developed and trained to bear the weight of her burden. Her tattered sandals flapped and scuffed on the steaming, sun-baked asphalt road.

As soon as the fish lady was permitted to enter through the gate into our backyard, we children would run to help lift the heavy basket from her head. She thanked us profusely for the help, quickly found a step of a box to sit on, then proceeded to rub her hot, weary feet. I studied her feet while she wiped the sweat from her face and body with a piece of red flannel that soon became saturated. Her long, flat, broad toes were spread wide, with discreet spaces between them, so that none touched—more like fingers when they are spread open, because she trudged endless miles every day with toes unconfined by shoes. A quarter-inch layer of thick, hard skin had formed under the soles of her feet, nature's way to provide a cushion, a shock absorber.

Our mama came outside to admire and inspect the collection of red snappers, sea bass, kingfish, parrotfish, and other nameless species. Her choice for the day was weighed on a rusty scale extracted from within the fish lady's basket. After serious negotiation for a price, Mama counted out the money, handed it over, and disappeared into the cool recesses of our house. The fish lady reached into the confines of her ample bosom and lifted out a cloth bag that was attached to her neck by a piece of string; she placed the money in the damp pouch and deposited it in front of herself for safe keeping. The fish were passed to Ettie the cook, who all this time had acted as a self-appointed consultant and arbitrator.

After we helped the fish woman replace the basket on her cushioned head, she thanked us for the help, the purchase, and the chance to rest. Once through the gate again, she swayed away down the street, crying out until her voice faded in the distance:

"Feesh! Feesh! Fre-esh Feesh!"

On another day, we might be visited by the silent vegetable-and-fruit man we called "Baboo" His white turban, rolled high on his head, made him seem tall and majestic, like a Maharajah. His shiny skin was the color of polished mahogany. A large, black moustache covered his mouth and hid part of his nose and cheeks. He was muscular and strong, so never accepted any help from us to lift the basket from his head.

Baboo looked like a real Indian from India, the progeny of indentured Indians who were brought to Jamaica as so-called "coolies" to do so-called "bitter work" as servants on the banana, coconut, and sugarcane plantations. They hardly ever intermarried, so preserved their customs, dress, and recognizable facial and physical features. In one pierced ear, Baboo wore a pea-size ball of gold that I always longed to touch. It glistened on the side of his head; I assumed it was the most valuable jewel in the world. His basket overflowed with treasures. I was never tired of catching my first glimpse of shiny, green avocados; purple eggplants; small, yellow pumpkins; ripe bananas and plantains; green, leafy lettuce; golden mangoes, and dimpled tangerines.

Baboo did not like anyone to touch his produce, so Mama pointed to the vegetables and fruits she wanted and Baboo passed them to the cook. Mama paid the coolie man, and the cook kept the vegetables; the fruits were taken into the house to be protected from hungry children. Up went the basket on top of Baboo's turban. The maharajah left as silently as he had come. We said of him, "Baboo can walk; Baboo don't talk."

Cakie, the pastry lady, arrived with a special box on her head, not a basket. The box was designed to display the contents and kept out flies. The four sides and the hinged top were made of glass, like an aquarium. My favorite confection consisted of shredded bits of coconut meat barely held together with brown sugar that crystallized around the little pieces. These "coconut cakes" were decorated on top with red dye. Another pastry consisted of molasses, baking soda, and flour baked in the shape of a disc; these brown buns, which we called "bullas," needed more than a little chewing but staved off hunger for long periods of time. I never could resist the little sweet and sour balls made from the flesh of tamarinds rolled in sugar.

The piece de resistance was Cakie's patties. A patty is about the size and shape of a croissant. A yellow envelope of pastry encloses a soft stuffing made from ground beef or chicken, seasoned with pepper and curry. A freshly baked patty retains its heat for a long time, so it seems like forever before one can dare to take that first bite. The warm contents ooze out as a delicious mixture. The patty remains a widespread favorite food, served hot from carts, shops, and restaurants in every corner of the island, especially at lunchtime. It is as traditional in Jamaica as hot dogs and hamburgers in the USA.

Our mother did not choose the pastry lady's offerings. We children chose. Mama just paid. She and the pastry lady chatted together while we rummaged through the box to choose our individual prizes. Cakie always gave me a small, sweet bonus, an item that had not been paid for. She was my favorite vendor, not only because I was allowed to choose the delicious things she sold, but also because she was a kind and friendly person.

Mary, the chicken lady, arrived with a basket that overflowed with a noisy, cackling flock of live chickens constrained in various ways. The wings of some birds were tied together, while the legs of others were bound with string. A few of them were not even tied, but immobilized by a special method of tucking the head and neck under the wings to blindfold and tranquilize them.

Hens, cockerels, and roosters of mixed heritage and varying stages of maturity shared the basket. The age of a bird could be estimated by the size of the comb on top of its head or the length of the spurs on the legs. The choice of a specific bird for dinner followed a painstaking and time-consuming process that lasted as long as an hour. Mary had to take each bird out of the basket so that we could squeeze, manipulate, and examine the entire body from beak to claw, even looking under the feathers to inspect the skin. Sometimes the color of the feathers and the length of the neck influenced the decision, as if these attributes would be related to the taste of the meat. Multicolored, iridescent feathers might on occasion prevail over solid colors like brown or white; but a well-bred Rhode Island Red was always the prime choice. It was Ettie, the cook's job to kill, pluck, and cook the chosen chicken.

Throughout the entire proceedings, the chicken lady adopted a patient, nonchalant attitude. Mary never complained or tried to speed up the deliberations. The live chicken would not spoil if kept from one day to another. I think she was amused by all the fuss; in any case, she enjoyed the chance to rest in the shade.

Sam the snowball man walked behind his four-wheeled wooden pushcart as if he was permanently attached to the two handles that protruded backwards. He usually wore shorts, a sleeveless T-shirt, and homemade sandals carved out of an old rubber tire. Every muscle in his body was on display, as if he had trained to win a bodybuilding contest. The patina on the ends of the hardwood handles bore witness to many years of pushing and pulling. He did not need to enter the backyard. He parked his cart outside on the street and was soon surrounded by thirsty customers.

On two opposing sides of the cart he had painted IN GOD WE TRUST. Each of the twelve letters was a different color and dimension, like a child might print them. The front panel was decorated with hummingbirds hovering above hibiscus and bougainvillea flowers. The rear panel advertised Sam's Snowballs.

Bottles of colored syrup were displayed on wooden shelves, and each bottle fitted perfectly in its own hole cut in the wood. One might choose the syrup by color, as from an artist's pallet, or by flavor. There was red for raspberry, strawberry, and cherry; yellow for orange, lemon, pineapple, and banana; green for lime and mint; cloudy white for vanilla; and clear for plain water.

A block of ice rested inside the cart, covered by a thick piece of rough, brown burlap for insulation. However, the drops of water that drained from underneath the cart advertised the rate at which the precious ice disappeared, melting away Sam's slim profits. He provided a few glasses in which he served the snowballs; Mama suspected they were washed infrequently, so we used our own glasses.

Sam pushed a shaver with a metal blade back and forth across the surface of the ice block, and with each push, the sharp blade collected a thin layer of ice. He tapped the back of the shaver on the cart every now and then to compact the fine, white shavings and lifted the cover to see if the shaver was full. When the shushing sound ceased, signaling that the proper quota of shavings had been collected, he shook them into a glass. He picked up the appropriate bottle and poured the chosen viscous, sweet liquid over the ice. I watched his performance with admiration, waiting impatiently for the tasty, cold snowball now turned red with my favorite strawberry syrup. It seemed that he shaved for too long and stopped pouring the syrup too soon. He stoppered the bottle, replaced it in a hole, covered the block of ice, collected his money, picked up the handles, and moved on.

A bell attached to the cart by a short piece of cord swung like a pendulum, and rang until Sam found his next thirsty customer.

Once in a while, a chimney sweep passed by. He was a mysterious, fragile man with a goatee and an aquiline nose. A few small locks of curly hair hung beneath his cap. He looked like the pictures I had seen of Haile Selassie, Emperor of Ethiopia, The Lion of Judah. He came along the street with quick little mincing steps, his black, long-handled brooms carried on his shoulder, his face and tattered clothes smudged with soot. As a child, I was terrified by his appearance. I feared that he might carry other children and me off to some dark, awful place from which I thought he might have come. So I hid behind the gate of our mini-fortress to watch him through a peephole. To tease him, I called out, "Hi, chimney sweep. Hi, funny chimney sweep." He never reacted, but just kept walking along proudly, as if he had to keep an urgent appointment to clean a kitchen chimney somewhere. His face pointed straight in front of him.

I do not recall seeing the eyes of the chimney sweep. I cannot remember ever looking into the eyes of any of those tired, toiling vendors. Even so, I still hear their plaintive voices and feel the weight of the burdens they carried throughout their wearisome lives. There was always a strong bond between us. They added excitement and joy to my childhood. I cared for them.

ETTIE BROWN

Ettie spent her whole life working from dawn to after dusk for a pittance, to serve the needs of all seven of us-father, mother, and five children. She had always been with us, since she, too, was but a child, living out her simple, fettered existence in a small, windowless room beside a hot kitchen. She was our servant out of necessity and circumstance, so we just demanded and commanded. After all, she was ours; she belonged to the family. We acted as if we owned her. But out of love and loyalty, Ettie became the surrogate mother of us all. She knew the family belonged to her. She owned all of us.

Ettie was a thin, shy woman who probably did not weigh more than eighty-pounds, and she seemed to be mostly sinews, with her smooth skin stretched tightly over a small, bony frame. What she lacked in size, she compensated for with energy, stamina, and strength. She made up for her lack of education with savvy, common sense, compassion, and love.

Her dark eyelids blinked rapidly all the time. Her eyes and body were in constant motion. Sweat always covered her--not beads of sweat, but just a thin layer that left her looking shiny and polished like a chestnut.

Ettie had bad teeth, and many of them were missing; she complained that they hurt. She smoked cigarettes in reverse, with the hot, lighted end placed inside her mouth. She could not talk then, but would salivate a lot, so the cigarette became wet and soggy. She explained that smoking that way prevented her teeth from hurting; it also stained her few remaining teeth brown. The air surrounding Ettie always smelled of tobacco and rum. When I was eight years old, she taught me how to smoke with the lighted end inside my mouth, too. I invariably burned my tongue and had to spit out the cigarette. We would laugh together at my failure.

When Ettie laughed or even smiled, she lit up our children's world; perhaps she lit up the entire universe. But when she sulked and pouted and put on her sad, angry face, my world was submerged in sorrow.

Ettie did more than cook and clean. She bathed me, cared for me when I was sick, and watched over me like a guardian angel. She acted as my nurse, my point of reference. I always sought Ettie's attention. "Ettie, look here.", "Ettie, I'm hungry.", "Ettie, find the ball.", "Ettie, tell me a story." It pains me that I cannot remember ever saying please or thanks to Ettie. She, on the other hand, had to adhere to strict rules of courtesy and respect. According to local custom, my parents insisted that when Ettie spoke to us children, our names should always be preceded by the word "mister" or "miss". Ettie could not read or write. If she had been able to spell, "mister" would have been "Missa". So Ettie always called me "Missa Ronnie." The way she said "Missa" became a term of endearment rather than a show of subservience.

Ettie's main job was to cook. The kitchen was set aside in the backyard, in a building separated from the house. The room had no windows and just one door. The floors and walls, made of red bricks encrusted and painted with soot, seemed hundreds of years old. There was no sink, no electricity, no refrigerator, no microwave oven, no propane gas, and no dishwasher except Ettie Brown. The only fuels were wood and charcoal, yet out of the cavernous oven and from the metal grilles and blackened, iron pots came tantalizing, aromatic odors of roasted meat and fish seasoned with curry, onions, and allspice--the most delicious gourmet meals that anyone could dream of.

Inside the kitchen, the temperature must have climbed often to 120°F or higher. But Ettie reigned there—our cook, our little kitchen queen. All her life, she seemed able to bear the unbearable, to sing when others might cry.

Three times a day, she struggled to start the fires, coaxing them to life with kerosene oil poured on kindling made from old newspapers. Her cheeks puffed in and out like bellows, encouraging the flames and keeping them alive. She cursed, complained, sweated, and chased us away to prevent us from spoiling the ritual. When Ettie began to hum and sing, it signaled that everything was under control. I would start to salivate, in anticipation of some superb dish about to be perfected. Nowhere, even in the fanciest restaurants of the world, have I ever tasted the equal of Ettie's fish, Ettie's pepper pot soup, Ettie's anything-to-eat. So, I have included some recipes.

Ettie also performed as our entertainer. She told unbelievable stories about her "true" experiences. Most of the tales described ghosts and other night creatures that appeared and spoke to her on moonlit nights in our backyard. Ettie never seemed to be afraid of them, even if they shook their swords and chains and made other threatening sounds. But I was afraid and huddled against her listening to the stories. I think that Ettie really lived among the ghosts and believed in them.

Ettie seldom went anywhere because she was either too busy or too tired. But every Saturday morning, she looked forward to shopping for our food in a nearby market. On those occasions, she dressed in the finest clothes she could put together, the hand-me-down shoes, dresses, and hats given to her by my sister. Ettie looked happy, pretty, and carefree on Saturdays. She left with a large, empty basket; she returned with a heavy load balanced on her head and the telltale odor of rum on her breath.

As far as I know, Ettie was never sick. No doubt the fires, the heat, the kitchen smoke, the cigarette smoking, the rum, the hard work, and the ghosts protected her. She lived to be about seventy years old, still wiry and without wrinkles or lines on her face or her boyish body. I say "about seventy years" because we did not know exactly when or where she had been born, or the identities of her mother and father. It was my mother who named her Ettie Brown.

Ettie is sitting sheepishly in a corner in heaven by herself, looking down with flickering eyes at the cigarette she is rolling, and smiling with pleasure that "Missa Ronnie" has stored her safely in his memory all these years. She is very happy that I have written her a story. Her smile is also lighting up that place. Ettie Brown's teeth do not hurt anymore.

Ronald E. Glegg

RECIPES

Rice & Peas

Ingredients:
*1/2 cup beans (kidney beans)
*1 clove of garlic
*1green pepper
*Scallions
*Black pepper
*Thyme, salt to taste
*2 cups of rice

Method:
Wash peas and soak in 2 cups of water in a pot for a few hours.
Cook peas until tender, adding more water if necessary.
When peas are cooked, add salt, whole pepper, black pepper, thyme, & scallions.
Let simmer.
Wash rice if necessary, then add to pot; mix everything together.
Cook on a low fire until done.

Escovisch Fish

Ingredients:
*5 whole small/medium sized snappers with the head and tail left on (also good with kingfish steaks)
*1½ tsp. salt
*1½ tsp. pepper
*3 garlic cloves
*Cooking oil
*White vinegar
*2 onions
*2 scotch bonnet peppers
*10 pimentos

Method:
Wash fish in vinegar and water
Dry fish in paper towel and place on a plate.
Cut small, deep gashes on each side of the fish
Rub salt and pepper on outside and in the gashes you made.
Place oil in a frying pan, enough to fry one side of the fish.
(This is not a deep fry; therefore, the fish should NOT be completely submerged in the oil)
Place 2 cloves of garlic in the pot and heat on high
Put a cinnamon stick in a pot of boiling water to alleviate the smell of the frying fish
Remove garlic cloves from pot
Carefully place fish on its side in the hot oil
Fry crisp and turn down the heat if necessary
Turn other side and fry crisp
Place fish on a plate with dry paper towels
Slice onions and scotch bonnet pepper
Place onions, scotch bonnet pepper, and pimento in a small pot with vinegar
Boil contents on stove for approx. 5 min. (Be careful of your eyes burning if contents are over heated.)
Pour contents on the fried fish for a hot and spicy flavor
The cooked fish can be stored in a fridge for several days to intensify the flavors.

Pepper pot Soup

Ingredients:
*6 stalks of celery
*1 small head of cabbage
*1small okra
*1/2 lb. pig's tail and/or ½ lb. salt beef
*Flour dumplings
* Yam or dasheen
*1 scallion
*1 Scotch bonnet pepper
*Black Pepper
*2 quarts water

Method
Boil meat and vegetables.
Puree vegetables and return to the pot
Add the sliced yam, sliced pepper, and other seasoning to taste
Add dumplings
Simmer for approximately one hour
Add black pepper
(Soup and Saturday go together in Jamaica.)

RUM LANE

Rum Lane marked the line that separated the poor from the middle class in the section of Kingston where I was born. The poor survived on one side in a slum, a barrio. It was home for the people who worked as "servants" to make life easy and comfortable for families on the other side.

The barrio contained huts and small houses haphazardly arranged on narrow lanes that sprouted even narrower lanes. Building materials consisted of anything available: wood salvaged from boxes; crates and packing cases; lumber begged or stolen; galvanized zinc sheets that might have been blown off a roof during a storm; panels and bumpers from discarded automobiles; a collection of unmatched shingles; even cardboard and boughs fallen from the coconut trees.

A profusion of small shops housed businesses. Cobblers repairing precious, old shoes, tailors straining their eyes to make sure where to place the needles; butchers with blood stained aprons; there were also bakeries, ice cream parlors, and laundries. The sidewalks adjoining these shops hosted many activities. Worn-out women sat on stools or boxes all day and into the evening, offering for sale their mangos, bananas, homemade pastries, and candies. Some of the younger women flounced around offering their bodies. Shoppers wandered around haggling for the last penny, as if their lives depended on it. Goats, chickens, and dogs scampered about, foraging for bits of edible discards. Naked and half-dressed children jumped, skipped, and played everywhere, begging for food and money. Roosters crowed and hens replied. Donkeys brayed; mules and horses clip-clopped as they dragged their creaking carts and left their dung behind them. Hundreds of bony, hungry, mangy dogs barked all day and through the night. Cats in heat screamed out their sexual needs and accomplishments. The barrio was never quiet.

My favorite place on Rum Lane was a nameless shop that housed a group of Chinese owners, consisting of only one woman but several men. This arrangement was dictated by the Jamaican laws dating from the early 1900's that restricted the number and sex of Chinese immigrants. As a result, the Chinese men and Jamaican women blessed the surrounding area with many children who had the telltale but attractive combination of dark brown skin and slanted, Oriental eyes. The Chinese people spoke little or no English to us, but they understood what we wanted to buy. I suspected that they also understood the strange, unkind, insulting things that were said about them. For instance, serious rumors claimed that they ate cats, dogs, and fat children. Their diet was in fact supplemented by ducks, chickens and pigeons, which I helped my father raise in our backyard. Everybody in our neighborhood shopped there.

Only the heads, necks, and shoulders of these short people could be seen, as they stood, silent and impassive, behind the barricade of high, wooden counters. This seemed so mysterious to me. Sometimes they sat on stools almost out of sight. Ready and quick to serve the customers, they moved about on the concrete floor like robots, shuffling in their leather slippers imported from China.

Every inch of the shop was stocked from floor to ceiling with supplies and groceries that did not require refrigeration. This included a variety of imported, canned goods, stacked neatly on the shelves to show off their colorful labels displaying pictures of the contents for those who could not read. The most popular items were corned beef, sardines, herrings, olives, peas, and peaches. An indispensable, irresistible ingredient of any shopping trip was a can of sweetened, condensed milk, that viscous concentrate of sugar and cream that we used in coffee, tea, and homemade ice cream. To the dismay of my mother, I would sometimes pierce a small, almost invisible hole in the can and suck it dry.

An open barrel of dry, salted codfish extended greetings with its unique odor that permeated the shop, the land, and the people. The grayish, flaky slabs of cod looked like pieces of dirty parchment or cardboard-stacked one on top of the other. The inexpensive codfish was a staple source of protein for the poor, and an occasional delicacy for middle class families who were also able to afford beef, chicken, and fresh fish. I would rip off small pieces of the codfish and chew it as a substitute for chewing gum. Too large a piece of the dry, salty fish absorbed mouthfuls of saliva, was difficult to swallow, and brought on an unquenchable thirst, which we claimed could only be quenched with several glasses of home-made lemonade.

Open cotton and jute bags rested on the floor displaying sugar, rice, and flour, each with its metal scoop on top, ready for serving. Yellow wheels of sharp Canadian cheddar cheese sweated and oozed their fatty liquids on wooden boards that sat on the counter, with sharp knives ready for cutting. Hams in their gauzy cloth coverings hung from the rusty hooks and competed for air space with bunches of bananas from which the shoppers selected as many fruit as they could afford.

Tall, covered glass jars protected hard and soft candies in all their tempting shapes, colors, and flavors. As a child, I stood in front of those containers hypnotized by the lollipops, toffees, jujubes, and conical milk chocolates in their silver wrappers.

Just beside the jar with red and white striped peppermint sticks stood my favorite candy, aptly named paradise plums. I would leave a few precious pennies on the counter and walk away with one plum in my mouth; a tight fist held the other six or so, wrapped in a small piece of brown paper that came from who knows where.

The shop stocked French wines, Spanish ports, sherries, rum, scotch, and other liquors from the world over. I tagged along with my father whenever he made that special trip to exchange his ducks and chickens for White Horse Scotch and Sandeman's port. I wished I were a friend of the man in the long, black coat posing on the label of the port bottle.

True to the name Rum Lane, men and women bought shots of rum in their own little containers in a bar nearby. Some started drinking early in the morning and continued throughout the day and night. As a consequence, customers who surrounded the place were sociable, talkative, noisy, playful, and sometimes intoxicated, belligerent, and uncontrollable. Policemen made frequent stops as they patrolled on foot to keep order and to discourage children and vagrants from lingering.

A special corner of the shop was set aside for a fifty-gallon drum of kerosene. The pungent oil was dispensed into a glass bottle or any other container brought by the customer. The bottle was plugged with a wad of old newspaper. The vapors escaped to leave behind peculiar, suffocating fumes that permeated the shop and Rum Lane. Kerosene was an essential commodity used to start charcoal and wood fires, and as the fuel for lamps. All over the island, those lamps created an eerie nighttime atmosphere as they shone like giant fireflies from windows and the doors of houses and shops, or flickered on sidewalks and in yards.

A constant medley of sounds and music could be heard throughout the barrio. Burley laborers dug trenches, singing old digging songs to set a steady rhythm as they lifted and lowered heavy shovels and pickaxes. A lone musician on the sidewalk or hidden away in a room somewhere sang solo, accompanied by the melodic thumping of his guitar. Popular lyrics told of a mongoose who ran into someone's kitchen and stole one of the best chickens, put it into the pocket of his waistcoat, and slid silently away, not realizing that the story of his crime had been broadcast all over the world.

My favorite song was *"Linstead Market."* It tells the story of a woman who takes food *("ackee")* to the market. No one buys anything (not even a *"quatties worth"*). Everybody keeps "feeling up" the food, and children linger *("linga linga")* to get a hand out. Meanwhile, she wonders how she will feed her own children.

Linstead Market
Mi carry mi ackee go a Linstead Market
Not a quattie worth sell
Mi carry me ackee go a Linstead Market
Not a quattie worth sell
Lord what a night, not a bite
What a Saturday night
Lawd what a night not a bite
What a Saturday night
Everybody come feel up, feel up
Not a quattie worth sell

Everybody come feel up, feel up
Not a quattie worth sell
Lord what a night, not a bite
What a Saturday night
Lawd what a night not a bite
What a Saturday night
Do mi mommy nuh beat mi kill mi
Sake a merry-go-round
Do mi mommy don't beat me kill
Sake a American rum
Lord what a night, not a bite
What a Saturday night
Lawd what a night not a bite
What a Saturday night
All di pickney dem a linga linga
Fi weh dem mumma no bring
All di pickney dem a linga linga
Fi weh dem mumma no bring
Lawd, what a night, not a bite
What a Saturday night
Lawd, what a night, not a bite
How di pickney gwine feed?

Boys and girls played their homemade musical instruments, improvised from metal cans, twine, wood, nails, pots and pans, and wooden flutes carved from bamboo. Record players blared hit tunes from shops and restaurants, and inspired people to dance in the lanes. Children sang their derisive children's songs, skipped rope, played hopscotch, and teased one another. Noise, music, and religion lifted the spirits of these trapped people and distracted them from their lack of everything else.

The barrio generated its own combination of odors. It smelled of fires, fumes, and the cooking of peanuts and codfish fritters, fish frying in sizzling coconut oil, brown rice steaming and bread baking. Smoke rose from round, black cast iron hibachis resting on the ground, dispensing the odors of burning charcoal and grilled food. The sickly sweet aroma of marijuana smoke drifted from secret places. The putrid smoke from smoldering garbage dumps insulted all the senses. Billy goats wandered through the lanes and spread their musky odor to attract the does.

The warm, sunny climate made living bearable in the barrio. Everything of any importance took place in the street and yards. But during the rainy season, misery and misfortune added to the pain of poverty. Sidewalk hagglers and the street vendors retreated to their humid, leaky rooms, losing their meager sales. Oblivious of germs and disease, children sloshed around in the dirty, muddy water that filled the lanes. Animals searched in vain for a dry spot in which to hide. The barrio perched on the edge of a gully. During heavy thunderstorms, the turbulent water rushed over the steep banks and carried away huts, trees, animals, and people to the sea two miles away, never to be seen again.

Resentment and frustration festered beneath the deceptively friendly surface of the barrio, waiting for a trigger to start an explosion. Rum and marijuana sometimes provided the gunpowder. Violence flared over seemingly petty matters, such as an insulting four-letter word, or if someone just brushed against another person, stared at someone for more than a few permissible seconds, or greeted another man's concubine or common-law wife. The worst offense was a reference of any kind to another person's mother.

Violence took all forms, from noisy curses and death wishes, to severe beatings with sticks, craniums crushed with stones, stabbings, death delivered from handguns, and heads severed from bodies with razor-sharp machetes.

As a natural consequence of the poverty, theft was the most common offense. Everything was fair game. Shops, stores, offices, and houses were plundered day and night. No object could be left unguarded. The local judicial system dealt severe punishments for even the smallest theft. A stolen chicken or a bunch of bananas might be worth hard labor for one year or more, depending on the circumstances and the magistrate. But nothing seemed to discourage the illegal adoption of other people's possessions.

Local standards placed my family in the middle class that made up a relatively small part of the island's population. Our neighborhood was comprised of about fifty homes, located just outside the barrio. Civil servants, teachers, office workers, and businessmen owned the houses. The neat, fenced yards and gardens stood in sharp contrast with conditions in the barrio on the other side of Rum Lane.

People came to Jamaica from many different parts of the world, including Africa, Europe, the Middle East, and South America. Because of the racial intermixtures, even within the same family, we ranged in color from black to white, with various shades of brown in between. All of the people in the barrio were black.

Our neighborhood, on the other side of Rum Lane, could not be described as integrated or segregated, friendly or unfriendly. Each family kept a respectful distance from the others. Friendly everyday greetings and conversations between our parents were not to be construed as an invitation to socialize or to visit one another. About forty children roamed and mingled in backyards on the street, but were not encouraged to enter each other's houses. We fought and played together. Our parents were distracted by their private thoughts about race, color, and superiority. Black was not beautiful in those days.

The poor and the middle class evolved together in a strained, symbiotic state. We struggled to find the balance between our mutual needs for love, respect, and human dignity, weighed against the forces of fear and prejudice. Rum Lane divided us into two camps, but connected and bounded us in one family, one world. The practicalities of life drew us together.

Early every morning, carpenters, painters, nannies, maids, cooks, washerwomen, and gardeners filed across the Rum Lane line to our side, to work for us. Late every evening, they trudged back across Rum Lane to spend the night in small, semi-dark rooms lit by kerosene lamps. The endless parade moved back and forth every day and night on a two-way road to nowhere.

Fearful, middle-class adults did not make casual or careless crossings into the barrio beyond Rum Lane. In reality, they had little fear, because the majority of the people who lived in the barrio were kind and courteous to us, although they were not as kindly to others in the slum. As a child, I moved about freely in the barrio. With childish naiveté, my brothers and I enjoyed the contrast in lifestyle and made friends there; friendships developed only between boys, never between girls. Middle class girls did not venture unaccompanied across Rum Lane, or if they did, only to pass through on their way to somewhere else. On such occasions, the girls marched along briskly, heads and noses held high, looking neither to the left nor right, no eye contact. Sometimes I walked my sister across the barrio in her little custom-made dresses, and we usually returned home before the sun went down. However, I think she observed the people, understood them, felt sorry about the way they lived, and empathized with them. But she did not speak to anyone.

As I wandered around the barrio, I often recognized some of the workers who came to our house. We exchanged greetings spiced with spontaneous humor.

"Hi man, how you doing?"

"Not so bad, sah."

"Not working today?"

"When you ever spy me workin'?"

"Over at my house on Lissant Road."

"Call dat workin'? When you fadah not lookin', me stop diggin' in de garden."

"I'm going to tell him."

"Don' do dat, you hear, sah. Lose me job."

"Just joshing. See you in the morning."

And I would walk away happy for the contact, feeling I had lightened his day.

The Chinese shop on Rum Lane typified hundreds of similar places distributed throughout the island. They all sold the same merchandise, gave off the same odors, and served the same shots of rum at any time of the day. Chinese owners segregated themselves behind impregnable metal shutters. For many people, the end of the day was signaled by the noisy clang of the shutters being rolled down to protect the shop from thieves over-night. The shopkeepers counted their money and sent some off to China. The middle class families carried on their smug, privileged lives. The poor went to sleep each night as neglected as the night before. Rum Lane fermented with discontent and unfulfilled expectations. The kerosene lamps never gave enough light to penetrate the thick darkness of tropical nights.

Papa's Motorbike

A heavy shower of rain in the early morning had spread a musty odor over Kingston, Jamaica. The city awakened after a humid night. Metal shutters were being rolled up in the commercial area. The banks, bars, shops, and restaurants were getting ready to open their doors for business. The stalls in outdoor markets were already uncovered, the wet cloth and plastic sheet covers had been stowed away under the makeshift shelves. Some vendors moved around slowly, sleepy-eyed; others sat on rickety chairs or boxes. It was time to go to work. The bell on top of the Kingston Parish Church struck eight times.

A stream of activity flowed towards the center of the business area around King Street. Carts and buggies rattled through the city behind their scrawny mules, donkeys, and horses. Electric streetcars screeched around corners as their metal wheels scraped against the steel rails that regulated the routes they had to follow. Impatient drivers of cars, motorcycles, overcrowded buses, and overloaded trucks revved their engines and sounded horns in frantic attempts to clear a path through the congested traffic.

The sky was still heavy with thunderclouds as sweating pedestrians scrambled to compete with the weaving bicycles and noisy vehicles for the limited space on narrow streets and lanes, stepping carefully to avoid the puddles of muddy water that had settled in the potholes. Policemen with white helmets and gloves risked their lives to direct traffic at some of the more crowded intersections. A larger-than-life statue of Queen Victoria perched high on a white marble pedestal in a grassy memorial park. She looked down on this colorful, congested, noisy scene with silent disdain, as she had done for many decades in the same hallowed spot.

My father roared away on his Harley-Davidson motorbike, as was his custom every morning, and headed for work downtown. Five minutes later, a truck came through a stop sign and smashed his left leg against the metal framework of the bike. Within a few minutes, a curious crowd gathered to study and analyze the awesome scene. Papa lay bleeding and unconscious on the wet, dirty asphalt street, and waited for a lifetime before an ambulance arrived.

Four days later, Papa regained consciousness in the Kingston General Hospital. This took place in the 1930's, before the invention of antibiotics. Iodine had been poured into the open wounds to prevent infection. He was lying bed, his left leg set between wooden splints, bandaged from head to toe because of the other wounds he had suffered all over his body. I could barely recognize my father the first time I was allowed to visit him. He held my hand, and I burst into loud crying.

The accident happened the same week that I had saved enough money to make my first major purchase. I bought a secondhand bicycle. I was a proud, joyful ten-year-old boy. The first night, I took the bicycle into my bedroom where it slept with me.

Uncle Jobie was my mother's favorite brother. He came to visit her at least twice every week, riding his shiny, sturdy bicycle that matched his six-foot tall frame. It was his only transportation. Each time he parked it in our backyard, he warned me, "Do not move it, do not ride it, do not even touch it." He meant it. But I disobeyed and learned to ride Uncle Jobie's bicycle during short, stealthy sorties while he was inside the house. The saddle was about at my shoulder level, and I did not dare to lower it. So I would put one leg under the bar, extend it between the wheels, and barely manage to get both feet on the pedals. This position required extra effort to maintain proper balance.

The many obstacles and obstructions in our backyard made it impossible to stay upright for more than thirty seconds or so. I had to steer around trees, the animals, and the house in a circuitous route, trying to maintain my balance. I spent more time on the ground than on the bike. The bike came down on me each time I fell, and I had to pray that Uncle Jobie had not heard the clatter. It was self-inflicted torture as the sharp edges of the metal pedals sometimes cut into my bare feet. However, after many of Uncle Jobie's visits and hundreds of falls, I mastered the skills to remain upright. I think Uncle Jobie was aware that I practiced on his bike, but he never said anything, never complained. He must have known all about the suffering that his bike and I endured during those months.

My brother Keith was seven years old when I bought my own bicycle. He had not experienced the pain and frustration of experimenting with Uncle Jobie's torture machine. He had not learned to ride yet. But the very first time he mounted my bicycle, he just rode away on it in perfect balance, a born, ready-made rider. I was astonished and hated him at that moment.

Difficult and unusual things came easily to Keith throughout his life. He played the piano by ~~air~~, no lessons. He taught himself some of the Chinese language, and mastered complex mathematics, physics, weaponry, and engineering. But ten years after I bought my first bike, as Keith and I rode home from a dance one night, without any lights, his bike hit a pothole. He fell and broke his collarbone. I wonder if that accident would have happened if he had learned the hard way to ride a bike, as I had, in the backyard on Uncle Jobie's monster. I wonder, too, if Papa's accident with the truck could have been avoided if he had waited for a few seconds before leaving home. Suppose it had started raining again before he left. Suppose I had just asked him a question, or told him I loved him. Perhaps he would have stopped to hug or kiss me, and the truck would have gone by before he reached the fateful intersection on his Harley-Davidson.

In those days, more than fifty years ago, our family was not explicit about declaring our love for one another. We must surely have shown it by our actions, but I do not remember that my mother or father, ever in my life said to me, "I love you." I am sure I never said it to them, but I know that we were bound together in a loving family of four sons, one daughter, and a devoted mother and father. This experience is quite different from present day relationships with my children, grandchildren, and my wife. Sometimes I am greeted with the question, "Have I told you lately how much I love you?" Nearly all partings and telephone calls end with the words, "love you," or "I love ya, miss ya." I have not yet learned to respond to this modern day salutation. I usually reply with just, "Thanks, me too," which I consider restrained and inadequate.

Perhaps in the present world so filled with hate, anger, and evil, we feel a more urgent need to declare love openly, frequently, to say it out loud so that someone hears, knows, and perhaps responds. An old adage teaches that actions speak louder than words; today, it seems to have been reversed to read words speak louder than actions.

My father had encircled our yard with tall fences and gates to keep out intruders. We lived with a certain sense of security in a middle class neighborhood, located near a barrio that supplied experienced prowlers and burglars.

One unforgettable night, after I had enjoyed about two weeks of non-stop riding on my new little bike, I made a critical error. I forgot to take my bicycle inside, forgot to lock it up; just leaned it up against the house outside my bedroom. The next morning, my bicycle was not where I had left it. I searched the yard, looked behind trees, and revisited every room in the house and the outbuildings that housed the bathroom, kitchen, and maid's quarters. My precious little black bicycle had disappeared. My magic carpet had flown or been carried away, by some wicked thief.

Next, I ran through the streets surrounding our home, crying, sobbing, hoping that someone had just borrowed it, and left it stranded somewhere nearby. That was one of the worst days of my life.

Papa lived in the hospital for about four months, while his broken left leg and other injuries healed. Our family spent sad and anxious days fearing that his leg might have to be amputated, because it had been so severely fractured. After the first month, the doctors said his leg was not properly set, so it had to be broken again and reset. We feared that he might die. As a ten-year-old boy, I thought about how unfair it would be to lose my father and my bicycle in the same period of my life.

As a result of the damage, Papa's left leg ended up about one inch shorter than his right leg. He was a proud man, handsome, vain, and careful about his appearance. He could not bear the thought of limping for the rest of his life—he was only thirty-eight years old. So, he designed a special boot with an elevated section constructed inside the heel, rather than adding a piece that would show on the outside. An expert local boot maker crafted the boots; always black, always from the softest, finest calfskin leather. Papa walked a lot everyday to conduct his business as a manufacturer's representative. He walked in public without a limp during his remaining fifty years. Although the fracture healed well, it left a deep, scarred dimple in his shinbone.

Papa's boots held a strange fascination for me. I volunteered to polish and shine them. I would always do the right boot first, perhaps to postpone the sad feeling of the raised section inside the left heel. I worked with diligence to produce boots that glistened, with the left boot always getting a little more attention than the right. Shining the boots was a special act of love, like looking after Papa, Papa's leg.

Our house was built on supports made of bricks and cement. So the floor was about two to three feet above the bare earth. The area under the floor was dark and mysterious, a perfect space to crawl into during games of hide-and-seek. Ducks and chickens made their nests, laid their eggs, and hatched their chicks on the dirt under the house without being molested. Months had gone by before I found my lost bicycle under the house. I never discovered who hid it there. It was the same day that Papa came home from the hospital walking with crutches. That was one of the best days of my life.

CABLE HUT

It was a harsh and treacherous place. My father parked our car about a mile from the sea on the south side of the island. No road led directly to the beach. We left our shoes in the car, and walked down a riverbed that was dry most of the time. We picked our way carefully among the smooth stones and round river rocks that looked like white pumpkins of all shapes and sizes. We avoided stepping on the stones, which were unbearably hot from baking in the oven of the tropical sun.

As we arrived at the shore, I rejoiced at the sight of coconut trees that protected a few thatched huts sitting exposed on the beach. The huts were dressing rooms and the only place to find some cool shade. A faded sign in large letters read: CABLE HUT BEACH.

The coarse, black sand absorbed the sun's energy and forced us to scamper across the hot surface to reach the water's edge. The sea roared and groaned, as if in pain. The waves broke on the shore with awesome force, their mouths filled and overflowing with froth. In an endless show of power, with a relentless rhythm, the sea attacked the land as if to destroy it. To a child, common sense said stay away, but with a cautious curiosity, and prodded by my father, I used to edge little by little into the water. The gravel, small stones, and the sand milled around my feet, back and forth as the waves moved in and out. It felt as if a hole might form and suck me in. As the millions of wet pebbles ground themselves against me and against one another, they gave off an ominous rattle.

I ventured about six feet further into the surf, standing in two feet of water, and the undertow took hold--an irresistible force that tugged at my feet and legs, then dragged my body twenty to thirty feet out into the tumbling water. Fear and helplessness caught hold when the sea took control. It felt as if it would never return my body to the shore. But the next incoming wave came to the rescue, dumping me in a rough and untidy manner; hard enough to cause severe abrasions on wet skin as it rolled my body like a toy over the pebbles. As I grew bolder, I wandered further out into the surf. The process was repeated over and over. I was scared and excited by the possibility that I would be ground to pieces and devoured by the sea.

My father knew how to swim out about 50 yards into relatively calm water, beyond the force of the breaking waves. He would stay out there for an hour or more at a time in the warm, salty water floating on his back, hands behind his neck, while I survived the battering of the waves. Sometimes I would spot sharks 100 yards out, their fins moving on the water like black sails. Gripped with frenzy, I would shout futile shark alarms to my father knowing that he could not hear because of the continuous roar of the sea and the fact that his ears were submerged. Even if he had heard me, my papa would have stayed out there floating until he felt good and ready to swim back to shore. This self-made man, headstrong, impulsive, and stubborn, lived his whole life that way-by his own rules and in his own time. When he decided it was time to go home, we found our hut and changed clothes.

As we were about to leave, the caretaker appeared out of one of the huts. My father reached into his pocket and handed over the few coins to pay for the use of the hut and beach, and for the homemade lemonade we drank. Then he handed the man an extra coin or two and thanked him for watching over our clothes. The leathery skin on the caretaker's hand imitated the color of the sand; his voice sounded like the gravel on the bottom of the sea.

"T'ank yu', sah," was all he said.

My father and I walked the hot mile back to the car.

It made me happy to see the car, to realize that once again I had survived the walk and the sea, and that sharks had not eaten my father. He was a religious man. The trip to Cable Hut Beach was like a pilgrimage, faithfully conducted after church on a Sunday, as an epilogue to the service. He never said much during the trip, as if speaking would break the spell. He looked refreshed and rejuvenated afterwards. I always wished I knew when I would go to Cable Hut again to risk my life and share the experience with my father, but that was a secret he kept to himself.

MAMA

I knew only one Granny, Mama's Mama. I remembered her well, because I spent happy, hilarious days and nights with her, in her home on Charles Street in Kingston. Stout, strong, and vivacious, she stood about five feet-three inches tall. Her wavy, light brown hair matched the color of her skin. A dark brown mole decorated her right cheek; I have one in the same place, so I know she was indeed my true granny.

Granny's family tree was shrouded in mystery, not a proper subject for casual conversation or questions. As a child, it seemed to me there must have been some special shameful secret to be protected. She was born in Jamaica about 1875, ten years after slavery was abolished there. Over the years, I never discovered any details about her ancestors other than that she was a descendant of African slaves and Europeans.

Columbus planted a Spanish flag on a Jamaican beach in 1494, then proceeded to torture and annihilate the native Arawak Indians who lived there a thousand years before he descended on them.

The English drove out the Spaniards in 1655, planted their flag, the Union Jack, then ruled for more than 300 years until Jamaica opted for independence in 1962. The island was a part of the British Empire before and after those cruel years when Granny was born and died sixty-three years later. Scottish soldiers wearing their colorful kilts were stationed in Jamaica. They were quartered in strategic locations to maintain order, to guard against invasion and rebellion, and to protect the ill-gotten possessions of absentee landowners. These lonesome men found companions among the local women.

Ships arrived with their ghastly cargos of African slaves; others brought Chinese and Indian coolies. They came on long journeys from Europe and elsewhere to exploit the slaves and the land. They came in a vain search for gold, then grew rich on sugar, molasses, and rum. Some stayed to dally with their lovers and concubines—their black African common-law wives. The Americans and Canadians later built their tourist resorts, mined the red bauxite earth, and converted it into aluminum. The descendants of all theses people, Arawaks, Asians, Europeans, Africans, North and South Americans, are now known as "Jamaicans."

Granny was a Jamaican. I am a Jamaican. I thank her for the potpourri of genes I inherited that made me strong and hardy, neither white nor black. I thank her for my thick, curly hair that has turned silvery and shiny in my old age.

Mama was the second of Granny's nine children. I grew up not knowing anything about my grandfather, not even his name. Mama was christened Gwendolyn Bodden. Granny's maiden name was Bodden—Mary Bodden. One memorable evening in August 1941, World War II was in progress and the German-Italian axis was scoring victories on all fronts. Our family discussed the war news every evening as we were gathered at the dinner table. I described the Germans as a dirty, barbaric group of killers. Mama took my sister, my older brother, and me to another room, leaving my father and two younger brothers at the table. She informed us that not all Germans were dirty and barbaric killers. For the first time, she revealed the identity of her father. And so, when I was twenty years old, I learned the name, nationality, and occupation of my grandfather. Mister Nedermeyer had been a German Consul in Jamaica when he met my granny, Mary Bodden. Mama was born out of wedlock from that union. Granny later married another man, became Mrs. Mary Lindo, and went on to become the respectable mother of seven Lindos.

Why do we all want to know where we come from? Why construct family trees to record the intermingling of our ancestors? Is it just curiosity or a more deep-seated drive to analyze and understand our past, present, and possible future? Is it a search for continuity, an exercise to establish identity, or simply a need to connect the links that chain all of us together? In

New Guinea, the heads of ancestors used to be coated with clay and decorated with cowrie shells. These heads were considered holy, and it was thought that they held the clan together in the past and present.

The study of genetics, including the central role of DNA, has provided knowledge of various factors that can influence our physical and mental capacity. Modern understanding of the chemical reactions that take place in the brain, blood, and body yield new methods to control and alter our emotional state. Antibiotics are tailor-made to combat bacteria that invade our bodies every moment of the day. Plastic surgery is a common device to remodel our appearance, to change and reconstruct facial and other features, to make us look young again. The process of aging can be modified so that we can walk, work, and live in a fashion not available to our ancestors. So we are able to keep in touch with our youth.

Like ancestral history, medical and pharmaceutical techniques have contributed another dimension of continuity. Our ancestral history adds length and breadth to our lives.

Mama's skin was white, smooth, and unblemished. Her round, moon-shaped face seemed always to be in repose. Long, straight, black hair fell lower than her waist. I enjoyed brushing it for her. Mama coiled her hair into a bun, worn on the nape of her neck. She was short, plump, and busty, like Granny. Being "fat" was not considered unattractive in those days; instead, some people regarded it as a sign of good health. Mama's upper arms were especially inviting, soft and resilient, perfect for hugging a husband and five children. Mama's lap had a special mother's shape, so it was easy and comfortable to sit on, impossible to slip off of. We children fought for the rights to Mama's lap.

Mama never raised her voice or shouted at us, and not necessarily because we were well behaved. She just acted and lived in a quite, subdued, calm manner that matched her voice and her face. She was not passive or resigned, just composed and in control of her emotions most of the time. However, when Mama decided to punish us, it was sometimes severe, something to remember.

As a child, I swore frequently, using all the known four-letter words, as well as other curse words invented and used in Jamaica. In several attempts to cure this habit, I was warned, spanked, grounded, and made to eat only bread and water for an entire day. Another dreaded sentence was to spend an eternity standing in a corner of the backyard with my left foot held up in my right hand, and my right ear held in my left hand. This balancing act, along with corporal punishments from my father, had little or no effect; I just kept on cursing, building a reputation for having a "filthy" mouth. Finally, one day when I was about eleven years old, the day of reckoning arrived. Mama and Ettie, the cook, both took hold of me after a wild cursing spree. They rubbed the inside of my mouth with hot peppers that grew in our garden. This was designed to purify my filthy mouth but instead it almost suffocated me. I stopped breathing. This reaction surprised and frightened them, so they worked frantically over me, flushing my eyes and mouth with water until I revived. Unfortunately, even this extreme attempt to sanitize my mouth had no lasting effect. I still swear compulsively, and as a result, my children do, too.

Mama played the piano well, so at an early age, we were exposed to a selection of classical composers. We grew up humming and whistling melodies from the works of Chopin, Mozart, Beethoven, Schumann, Schubert, Strauss, and others. Mama would adjust the mahogany piano stool to the proper height, and then sit like a queen in front of the black upright piano in the parlor. We gathered around her like loyal, admiring subjects and fought for the privilege to flip the pages in the music book. We could not read music, so Mama signaled with a quick nod of her head when she was ready for the next page. The heat always bothered her, so one of us was assigned the task of fanning her with a wooden-handled cardboard fan while she played.

On these musical occasions, as I sat close to Mama on the piano stool, I loved to smell the soft fragrance of "Coty" powder, her favorite perfumed dusting powder, which she patted all over her body with a thick, fluffy puff. Sometimes she would deliver a sudden mischievous pat of powder full in the face of any unsuspecting child nearby. We tried to dodge that playful pat because it was difficult to breathe through the cloud of power. I still recognize those boxes of Coty powder displayed at cosmetic counters today. Then I recall that similar box sitting open on the dressing table in Mama's bedroom, a puff on the top of the powder, ready for Mama.

Every person has some attribute by which they can be recognized and remembered, like a signature. It might be a way of walking or speaking, the twitching of eyelids, lips, or nose. My wife continually rearranges her hair behind her ears or twirls small skeins of hair between her fingers. My son behaves in a peculiar manner at the end of a phone conversation. In order to not break off contact prematurely, while keeping the phone at his ear, he moves his head sideways and downwards until it almost touches the table or desk where the base of the phone is located; only then does he say goodbye and place the phone in its cradle.

Mama had her signatures, too. She wore white dresses with pleats in the front, sewn by her own dressmaker. She craved chocolates. At her request, the fatty little nob at the furthest end of a roasted chicken, known as the "parson's nose", was always reserved for her. Mama reacted instantaneously to the smallest amount of wine; her entire face became flushed and red, lasting for a few hours. On festive occasions, we waited anxiously for the moment that Mama would raise the wine glass to her lips, in order to witness this astonishing phenomenon.

In the 1940's, Mama and her doctors were not sufficiently aware of the dangers associated with high blood pressure, elevated cholesterol levels, and being overweight. She just looked pink and healthy to us. One afternoon, as she sat in her rocking chair on the porch, blood vessels broke in Mama's brain. My father had the presence of mind to place a spoon in her mouth so she could not destroy her tongue as she experienced what he thought was an epileptic fit. The stroke left her bed-ridden and partially paralyzed. Spinal taps were done to study her condition, but did nothing to relieve or improve the situation. She remained quite cheerful, however, and was able to converse in a normal voice. Her memory seemed unimpaired.

As I sat at her bedside one morning, suddenly her body went limp and the blood drained away from her face, leaving it white and chalky. I heard a sound never to be forgotten, a succession of noises in her throat like those of a baby's rattle. A great silence fell, as if all sounds and sensations had been banished from the world. She was only forty-six when her spirit left her body. There is no way to describe the experience at that moment when you are the only person present at your mother's death. Scream, shout, smile, laugh, cry, pray, hug, hold, run, die?

The sound of the rattle is recorded in my brain forever; it plays over and over, a dirge, an accompaniment for a break in continuity. A link broke; the chain snapped.

A LETTER TO MRS. MURRAY

Dear Mrs. Murray,

I was five years old when I fell in love with you. You lifted me, wrapped your arms around me, hugged, and kissed me. Your soft right hand encircled my small fist and guided it, teaching me to write on my first day of school. I remember that you smelled so fresh and fragrant.

Mrs. Murray adored children and had four of her own—three girls and one boy.

I was in love with your three daughters, and thought they were beautiful. They were older than me and acted as if they were my sisters, playing jacks, marbles, and any other games they could think of. Your son, Eric, was a good friend and playmate. I wonder what he is doing with his life now.

Eric appeared at our house at any hour of the night or day, and my family looked forward to his frequent visits. I enjoyed his talent for relating detailed replays of the movies he had seen, especially those about cowboys and Indians. Eric saw every Fred Astaire-Ginger Rogers's movie, and would sing and dance as he retold a plot; that's how I learned to tap dance. We all felt obliged to learn the lyrics just to keep up with Eric. He played with the little finger on his left hand, fidgeting with the short, extra mini-finger that grew there.

A part of Mrs. Murray's backyard was adjacent to an open-air movie theater. At night, several of us boys would climb to the top of a tall tree so that we could see into the theater from above,

100 yards away. Tiny figures moved in aimless silence across the screen; we were too far away even to hear the sound, yet we thrilled at seeing a free show.

> *I recall your meticulous speech, every word pronounced in proper and clear diction, as if you were rehearsing for an elocution contest. I can still see your expressive face as it transmitted every emotion you felt sadness, joy, annoyance, disapproval, or disgust. You could have won an Oscar for best actress.*

By my calculations, Mrs. Murray was born about 1880, so she was of the Victorian era with its emphasis on strict rules and reserved behavior. And yet she was a vivacious lady who loved to sing and dance, and would have enjoyed life in the 2000's, with its freedom of expression and creativity.

Mrs. Murray was a middle-class aristocrat, born to an English physician and a Jamaican teacher, both of whom instilled in her a sense of discipline, a love for knowledge, and the elements that would shape her life. She had never traveled outside the island of Jamaica, but she assimilated European ideas and customs. Her immaculate clothes were sewn by her own dressmaker from fashionable fabrics and patterns.

Gardening was one of Mrs. Murray's hobbies; roses and chrysanthemums thrived under the directions she gave to her gardener. She had a keen sense for the nuances of classical music. She kept a piano in her house. She did not know how to play it, but many friends kept the keys busy.

> *I think about the precious years spent with other children in your little private school on Blake Road. I still see you moving around the classroom to coach, monitor, scold, and inspire us. The values you taught us have lingered with me throughout my life to try hard, to keep learning, to do my best, and to be kind to people. I can hear myself reciting multiplication tables with you, over and over until I got it right. Your firm and bossy manner was tempered with love. I was privileged to be one of your children.*

Not everyone was admitted to Mrs. Murray's private school, a small, elite establishment with a specified limit on the number of children, and only two or three teachers beside herself. She alone decided who would attend the school, based on her intuition, prejudices, and personal judgments.

The assessment started with her evening visit to the family home to converse with parents and to observe the children, like a friendly social worker. She made her own private estimates of the family's financial and social status, and measured the child's intelligence, behavior, and potential. She chose with care, perhaps she even discriminated, because most of the chosen were of lighter skin color. However, this methodology allowed her to maintain rigid standards of behavior and scholarship for about fifty children.

Mrs. Murray was a friend of my mother and father. They sat together on our porch, drank lemonade on hot evenings, and talked about adult things that I never heard. I always had to appear at some appropriate moment dictated by my mother, to wish Mrs. Murray good evening, talk to her for a few minutes, and be as well behaved as possible. When I became five years old, she invited my parents to let me attend her school. She devoted her whole life to being an inspired and inspiring teacher of children, conducting her own private school in a firm and business-like manner, with wisdom and autocratic perfection. She prepared me for learning, for appreciation of the arts, and for an interest in science. "Mrs. Murray's Preparatory School" was an appropriate name in every meaning of the words.

I want to thank you for all the subtle and overt ways in which you prepared me for growing up, for life, for the future. I understand now what created the nucleus for my appreciation of music, drama, dance, and beauty.

Mrs. Murray sent away to England for scripts of plays written for children. Each year, one play was presented in a public theater for one night only. She functioned as the producer, director, choreographer, costumer, make-up artist, and stage manager. The plays were usually set in enchanted forests inhabited by elves, fairies, princes, and princesses. The staging required ingenuity. For instance, in order to simulate the season of fall, which she in fact had never experienced in the tropics, she instructed us to gather dry leaves for days before the play, take them in bags to the theater, and scatter them on the stage. Fireflies danced around with flickering, battery-operated lights attached to their costumes.

Mrs. Murray taught parents to make costumes and trained children to sing, dance, and act. The lyrics were set to classical music such as the Liszt Hungarian Rhapsodies, which I still hum from time to time. A professional orchestra was hired for the occasion, and the entire production would have been fit for off-Broadway. After the play was presented, an exhausted Mrs. Murray retired to bed for about one week of complete rest.

Do you remember Austin, the tall, skinny boy with a big voice for a ten-year-old? It seems so long ago. You decided he would be the prince in the last play before we left your school. I wanted that part so badly. Instead, I got the role of the wicked wizard. In the last scene, Austin and I fought that fatal duel. His cardboard sword passed between my arm and body, and I fell dead among the dry leaves that we had strewn on the floor of the stage. Thanks to your early training, Austin and I have had successful careers. We discovered one another a few months ago at a meeting of the American Medical Association. We talked about you, Mrs. Murray, remembering your commitment to perfection, and how you preached and practiced discipline, scholarship, and love. I still envy him for the role of the prince.

It took five minutes to walk from my home to the school in Mrs. Murray's 20-room mansion. She lived there with her husband and their four children, her brother, and mother. Just to be in Mrs. Murray's house and spend time with her family was like living a scene out of a movie. Her house was a window on the world, where her friends, the other students, and their parents formed an exciting procession.

Her brother, Bertrand, was ill, but as children, we were not permitted to ask what was wrong with him. He owned an unusual electrical machine that always aroused our curiosity, so we gathered around to watch him use it. After he plugged it into an outlet and adjusted some knobs on the black box, he would grab hold of two metal handles that buzzed and vibrated like a present-day massage machine. He shook himself with it for hours each day, trembling all the time. It was a form of entertainment for me; especially since now and then I was allowed to take hold of the handles and tremble, too. I don't think the treatment did him any good.

In closing I want to let you know I treasure the fact that our affection for one another has grown and lasted for all those years since I graduated from your school as a ten-year-old. It was due to your continued mentoring that I won the scholarship to a private school. I hope you are happy to be retired, even though it means giving up your school. But now you have more time for your roses.

I think of you often; especially now that summer has surrendered to the chemistry of fall. I am looking at my garden through the window in my study. Roses and chrysanthemums are blooming. The lawn is like a green platform. Small, happy children are playing out there. It is ready for actors. Dry, multicolored leaves are drifting down to decorate the stage.

Love,
Sincerely   Ron

DEVIL'S LEAP

Cane River Falls is a secret place about five miles east of Kingston. Cool, clear water oozes out of a crack in the hillside, tumbles about fifty feet into a circular basin, then disappears underground. Over time, a rocky plateau has been eroded by the constant flow of water. A deep, natural pool has formed, wide enough for diving and swimming. The water is green, reflecting the color of the ferns and the canopy of surrounding trees rather than blue sky. Flat ledges of rock protrude at various levels above the water and provide solid platforms for divers. One special ledge about thirty feet high was reserved for the more daring and experienced divers. We boys named it Devil's Leap.

I rode to the falls on my bicycle with my fourteen-year-old friend Maurice. His younger brother Dudley tagged along. Maurice and Dudley lived next door to me. Across the road from our houses, a large piece of undeveloped land was surrounded by an ancient, rusty, galvanized zinc fence six feet high and guarded by a creaky iron gate. It was known as Clovelly Park. We always found a way to sneak in and roam around to chase lizards, play games, climb trees, and smoke cigarettes. The soil was so hard and dry that the grass could hardly survive. However, at certain times of the year, buttercups grew in profusion, decorating the field with a carpet of yellow, cup-shaped flowers. Bees congregated in that golden haven. The ground would come to life as thousands of bees flew from flower to flower and filled the hot air with a constant buzzing.

Maurice had mastered a special trick; with a super quick movement, his hand would dart out and catch the fluttering wings of a bee between his thumb and forefingers, and then gently released the little captive, unharmed, to continue its busy search for pollen and nectar. Only rarely did he collect a sting instead of a bee. Maurice excelled at everything he did.

The three of us arrived at the falls hot and sweaty, threw down our bikes, and raced to the pool in anticipation of dunking in the cool water. We dove a few times from the lower ledges, progressing higher and higher, until I decided that I was not daring enough to go further up. Maurice, however, announced that he would try to dive from *Devil's Leap.*

I shouted to him, "Maurice, forget about it. Come on down."

Dudley called out, "Maurice, don't be a fool."

He did not follow our advice. A few minutes later, he stood there, looking down at us from thirty feet up, smiling, making up his mind to jump. He was tall and strong for his age. For a while, he posed there, erect, flexing his muscles, then executed a perfect swan dive right into the middle of the pool. Dudley and I waited for him to surface so that we could applaud in unison. The ripples in the pool settled down. We waited an eternity, staring at the green water. Maurice never came up. We were stunned. I was paralyzed with fear. Dudley's face was as white as chalk when he asked, "Where the hell is he?" and I replied, "Oh, playing games again."

I swam carefully down into the pool many times to search for him, holding my breath as long as I could on each try. With each search, I became more desperate. After another eternity, I realized I would not find him. The pool had swallowed our Maurice, my best friend.

Two hours later, some men arrived with a grappling hook tied to a stout rope. They dragged the hook back and forth across the pool in a systematic manner, fishing for Maurice. After many futile attempts, the slack in the rope tightened, and one of the men called out, "I t'ink we got 'im." We watched as Maurice was pulled out of the pool dripping pink water. The men agreed that he must have struck a rock with his head, and then was trapped between two ledges under the water.

Dudley and I looked at the slack, wet body laid out on the rough, gray rock and then at one another with disbelief. Neither of us knew what to say or do. I stared at the raw, red wound where the hook had caught on Maurice's arm. I looked at his open eyes, but they could not respond. The drops of water on his smooth, brown cheeks make it seem as if he had been crying. Does everyone cry before they die?

I was fourteen years old. It was the first time I had ever seen a dead person.

The men started to breathe into Maurice's mouth and push on his chest. I prayed that he would say something, maybe even move a little. I had always seen Maurice in motion, had watched him run, swim, catch bees; I had heard him laugh, shout, and sing. I looked at his eyes again, afraid, and started to sob. It did not seem fair that my friend had been taken away from me so suddenly, so simply. I was not prepared. Grief walked unannounced into my life, accompanied by guilt. I felt that it was my fault. I should somehow have prevented the accident, climbed up and stopped him from diving.

Death does not announce its arrival, does not ring the doorbell, does not make a telephone call, send a greeting card, nor compose an e-mail. It snakes in through the cracks in our armor or cruises in like a stealth bomber. We cannot declare war on death. We must sign a treaty and try to make peace with it.

No matter when a deathblow strikes, we are never prepared for the first shockwaves that slam into us. No matter how many times it invades our personal lives, each time death will break down the door and let in the demon grief again. It makes no difference whether we are young or old, whether we are told the news or witness the final event ourselves. Death will always cause a commotion and shatter the peace.

The grim statistics of death reach us every hour, everyday through newspapers, magazines, radio, television, and the Internet; Cain kills Abel, an assassin's bullet destroys John F. Kennedy, and a child drowns in a neighbor's swimming pool. Only one of the 302 passengers survives the crash of an airplane. A celebrity dies of complications from AIDS, and 2,000 people lie entombed under buildings leveled by an earthquake. At the battle of Iwo Jima, 6,821 American soldiers sacrifice their lives. The Holocaust devours millions of Jews, and Albert Schweitzer dies in Africa. Terrorists kill 3,000 people in New York's World Trade Center. The list goes on forever and ever to record the victims claimed by murder, accidents, disease, natural disasters, wars, genocide, and old age. My friend Maurice drowns in the green water at Cane River Falls.

As each installment of deathnews reaches me, I feel an immediate rush of sadness. I remember the death of Maurice and the deaths of all the people that I have loved. I ask the universal question, "WHY?"

I substitute myself for one of the victims. For instance, I try to imagine what I would do and think during the thirty seconds as the airplane spirals before crashing into the earth at six hundred miles per hour. Contemplating the horror, I feel pain, physical pain, but not grief. Grief waits in the aisles for the arrival of another person to inflict intense emotional suffering after the death of a mother, a father, a sibling, a mentor, a friend.

Now, fifty years since Maurice drowned at Cane River Falls, I love but fear the water. It haunts me. I keep remembering the green water. I choose to live within sight or easy reach of a lake, the ocean, or a swimming pool. I need to be in touch with the beauty and danger of water. I swim quite well, but after a few strokes, my strength begins to drain away, flows into the water, leaves me weak. Sometimes I panic, so I always stay close to the edge of the pool just in case. I have taken lessons to conquer the fear, but it persists. I am afraid of drowning.

On the day that Maurice's funeral procession left from his home, a solid carpet of yellow buttercups covered Clovelly Park; but there were no bees.

PASSAGE TO FREEDOM

I have been held captive for many months. The compartment is warm and dark; the walls are wet and slippery. Tied to a wall by a short cord, I can hardly move around in the small area. I cannot remember how I arrived here, or exactly how long I have been confined. At times, it seems that I am being transported by some invisible entity. At other times, I feel unconscious, blank, unfocused, as if I am floating upside down, tumbling in space, not able to breathe.

A series of regular, monotonous beats continuously break the muffled silence of my prison. Boom-boom, boom-boom, boom-boom, on and on, boom-boom. Someone trying to attract my attention? Another prisoner banging on the walls? A musician playing on the drum? Something thumping on my cocoon? The beat of a giant heart? There is no way to solve the mystery. I am out of direct contact with the world. My brain is not functioning properly.

I am fed only through a tube; the liquid food must be nutritious, because my weight increases steadily. Hidden forces work to cause subtle changes in my appearance and behavior. My head feels large compared with my arms and legs. The confinement becomes more oppressive, the enclosure more restrictive. I have a compulsive need to exercise, to kick my feet, curl my toes, move around impatiently. My entire body feels as if it is submerged at the bottom of the sea, with no way to escape the pressure, although I struggle to rise to the surface.

The aimless, frantic fidgeting stops whenever melodious sounds ripple through my cage. Faint whispers from far-off voices mingle with the pleasing overtones of musical instruments. The rhythmic tunes and harmonious songs bring enchanting interludes of complete relaxation, and a promise of relief. I pay close attention to the concertos and sonatas; the music stimulates my brain, keeps me feeling more alive, and relieves some of the pressure and anxiety.

The pressure grows stronger. The bones in my head are beginning to hurt, as if a clamp encircles my skull to crush it. Crackling sounds accompany the compression. The pain is almost unbearable. I feel as if I am being crushed, smothered, and stifled; the agony tests my will to survive. I have to be courageous.

A small part of my brain sweeps back into my distant past, receiving messages of timelessness. My mind drifts freely on a voyage through all the ages of man. The luminous figures of ancient gods and goddesses appear in a procession, looking down with compassion. The vision fills me with awe and anticipation. The experiences evoke a sense of déjà vu. Have I been through all of this before? Am I revisiting an old, familiar realm?

My head aches. Through the delirium and the pain, I muster just enough strength to utter a silent cry for help. Will someone give me the courage and strength to bear the pain?

Suddenly, the crown of my head senses a draft of cool air. My skull moves slowly through a tight, hard, dark shaft. My body turns, wriggles, spirals like a corkscrew. The crushing and squeezing continue unabated, an elastic band is stretched tightly around me. The pressure is on my neck and shoulders now. Something grasps the top of my head, pulling it gently but firmly, trying to guide me out of the tunnel. Spasmodic forces push from inside the narrow passageway. My spine is twisted and bent. I cannot endure more pain.

Mercifully, the band snaps, the grip of the vise loosens. My head emerges from the trap. But the exit is too small for the rest of my body. Waves of claustrophobia engulf me. Heat rises to my scalp. My eyes feel as if they will pop out. I try to scream, in a bold attempt to escape from the suffocating dungeon.

Then the miracle takes place. Torso, arms, legs, feet, all the limbs follow one another, slipping out of the lubricated mold. I am overcome by the feelings of intense pleasure. I am free at last, released from captivity. The titanic struggle has ceased.

The cord that tied me to the wall is cut. I dangle by the heels, head down, enormous pressure relieved. I am naked and wet. The air in the large chamber is dry and cold.

I am choking. A tube inside my mouth sucks out the mucus, the viscid secretion that moistened and protected me during all those months in the cave. At last, my throat is clear. I make a slight movement with my mouth, and emit a quiet wheeze. Is it a sigh of relief? A gasp? No. With a mighty effort, I have drawn in air through my mouth and nostrils. It burns. I quiver, shudder. Millions of tiny tubes and sacs inflate my chest.

My lungs puff up like balloons. The expansion produces another torturesome but momentary pressure. I can breathe.

My eyelids open for a fraction of a second, then close to protect the eyes from the unaccustomed glare of the bright light. Something forces the lids open again. Watery drops hit the eyeballs and drain to the corner near my runny nose. The liquid attacks my naked eyes, sets them on fire. So I squeeze them shut again. Simultaneously, I hear a click followed immediately by a brief and dazzling flash. The light penetrates through the closed eyelids. I squint in response to the sudden shock. I feel eyelashes close against my wrinkled face, like the gentle landing of a butterfly.

A chaotic mixture of sounds vibrates from all directions. The shrill clatter assaults my eardrums, and creates another ache inside my head. I move both hands together in jerky motions to cover my ears and shield my eyes, trying to block out all the intrusions. But the thunder rumbles on, and the lightning flashes.

My vocal cords dilate. I can make my own sounds. So, I open my mouth as wide as I can and cry out. All the noises mix with the bawling and fuse into a startling pandemonium.

I smell the acrid fumes from the black ink used to record my footprints, and feel the sticky residue on the soles of my feet.

These are too many traumatic experiences, too rich, too frightfully intense for one body on one day. I cry out again and again. Tiny, pear-shaped drops roll down from the corners of my eyes. Tears flow for the first time; tears stream for the pain intermingled with the pleasure of my birth. Tears are shed for passing through the abyss, for joining the world, and for the memories of prison.

Was I so caught up in the struggle to escape, that I have forgotten the comforts of my mother's womb? Where has all the tranquil darkness gone? Where is the blissful, nurturing warmth that surrounded me all those months?

I miss the rhythmic thumping of our two hearts playing their duets. I long for the reassuring creaks of her joints, the murmurs of her breathing, the rumblings of her stomach, and the gentle swaying of her body. I yearn for the whispers, the ethereal music, and the serene filtered light that permeated the lake of amniotic fluid.

I have been bathed and massaged. A warm cloth is wrapped tightly around me. The delicate membrane of my skin recoils from the small, sharp points that protrude like thorns from the fabric of the swaddling blanket. Little prickles itch all over my ultra sensitive body.

Despite all the discomfort, I collect my thoughts. I can breathe. I can see and hear. I can cry. I can taste salt in my tears. I feel my heart pulsating, pumping blood through my body. I can smell. I can suck my finger. The eternity of my incarceration is complete. I am alive.

In celebration of my life, I move in synchrony with my mother's voice and recall the times I danced in her womb to the beat of our hearts; the beats that lulled me to sleep, and awakened me as well.

I am placed on my mother's stomach. Instinctively, I inch my way along her body and finally touch her breast. I snuggle and suckle, while she strokes and caresses my fresh body with soft, soothing fingers. With my head resting on her chest, I hear the measured drumbeats of her heart again, and retrieve some of the memories of the first world in which I lived.

We looked at each other up close, two old acquaintances reunited. We are bonded together, continuing a process that started in the womb several months before. I enjoy the protective shield of her love. I feel wanted, accepted, cherished.

Exhausted, I fall asleep in her arms, and dream my own dreams.

POOR SARAH

Sarah lived to be seven years old. When we picked her up, none of us realized the agony we would go through during those years. We chose her from a litter of five, one wintry afternoon in an untidy kitchen in an old farmhouse. Her mother greeted us at the driveway with a ringing, penetrating bark, menacing, dirty white, and smelly. She should have been a warning. Four of the litter slept peacefully, while one tumbled around trying to get the attention of the others, by stepping all over them and nipping at them. That's the one we wanted. The farmer's wife told us how terribly sweet that particular one was, what a nice round tummy she had, but how it was just so much work to keep them all.

"What's her name?" we asked.

"No name yet," she said

So we took her home and named her Lady Sarah. We had the space and a yard, and we thought we wanted a dog.

Sarah was not-quite-pure-old-English-sheep-dog. While she was a puppy, we kept her in the kitchen in an old playpen with a net around it. At night, she would climb up somehow and be on the kitchen table when we got up in the morning. Sometimes she fell off the table and ran around the kitchen looking like a little lamb. For a time, she wore a diaper because it seemed she would never be housebroken.

We had visions of bringing up a dignified, slow-moving, longhaired dog that would lie peacefully by the fireplace, like you see in movies. When she grew up, people who weren't scared of her thought she was cute, a dog without eyes because they were covered with lots of hair. We would let her run in the field behind a neighborhood school; happy with the way her hair flew in the wind. We took turns walking her; we pretended she was heeling, but she was really running ahead of us, pulling our arms out of their sockets.

She liked to have her picture taken and would sit up looking big and plump with all that hair, wagging a tail she did not have and showing off her red, wet tongue. She was a dog that should be seen, but could *not* be trained. We took her to an obedience school, and she attacked the teacher the first night. She was expelled from the class. It made us cry. One tends to take these things personally, especially when the teacher told us to destroy her.

When she was six months old, she ran away from home and returned with one leg torn apart by an animal trap in the neighbor's yard. The vet fixed it up as well as he could, but Sarah would not leave the scars alone. So she developed some festering sores. We all loved her, even our cat--from a distance. The difference between a dog and a cat is that a dog can really love you. I am sure Sarah loved us. I would know it when we brushed her hair or looked after her leg, bandaging it year after year.

She lived in exile in the doghouse I built for her in the garage. Sometimes, especially after cold winters, her hair had to be trimmed. It grew so thick that no comb or brush would move through it. Her body was amazingly frail without hair, and it always seemed as if she was embarrassed to be seen in such a state.

There were the children, too, while we had Sarah. She was a part of our lives and our family, and protected us from visitors and strangers with her ringing bark. She had an acute sense of hearing, and it would drive her crazy to hear a window being opened. One year, when we all decided Sarah was too much for us, our daughter and I decided to leave her at an animal shelter, hoping some new owners would have the physical strength and patience to spend more time with her than we did, perhaps train her. Our guilt was mounting about always having her leashed and not allowing her to spend time in the house. After we signed her in and paid our fee, our daughter and I walked back to the car holding an empty leash, not wanting to show each other that we were crying.

"All right," I said, "let's go back and get her."

So we drove home, Sarah on the back seat slobbering and whining, with scared little eyes behind her matted hair. We resumed cleaning up her mess, having her hair trimmed, having our arms pulled, our fingers twisted and hurt in the leash, patting her and loving her.

The last summer, things did not go too well for Sarah. Her sore leg was getting worse. Repeated trips to the vet did not do too much good. The bandages would be bitten off within a few days. We devised all sorts of things to keep it protected with plastic bags, casts, old socks, all to no avail. She was beginning to limp badly and did not run too much anymore. She would just look up rather disturbed when we came to clean or feed her. Sometimes, on our insistence, she would sigh, pick herself up, and limp to her dish. The vet said the leg was cancerous and should be amputated. We weren't ready for that.

We said to ourselves: "It's just a dog," but the thought kept us all awake some nights. Her eyes were beginning to look redder. I never knew if it was pain or the realization that we did not know what to do for her.

"Oh, I can't believe what's happening," cried my daughter. "Damn it, that dog never hurt anyone."

"Sarah had an all right life," I said, "and at least we loved her and she loved us." It was good to feel tears on my face as I scratched Sarah's head.

My daughter cried, almost chanting, in a steady, vibrating tone.

"What a rotten life this is," she cried, "to have to make such a decision," and she banged her knees with her fists in frustration. We both got up and walked in different directions, swearing and slamming doors. That evening, I went to say goodbye to Lady Sarah, knowing that the following day we would take her to the vet to "put her to sleep." I pulled her hair and ears away from her eyes. It seemed as if she winked at me. I got a blanket, wrapped her up, and went to bed. All night, I saw her in front of me. The next evening, the family walked around with swollen eyes. For months, we thought we heard Sarah bark, especially when we opened the windows.

The Cowboy Hat

Eight-year-old Ian ran over to me with a photo album.

"Grandfather, who is this old man in the picture with a big, white moustache and a cowboy hat?"

"Ian, that's your great-great-grandfather."

"My whaaaat?"

"That gentleman was your mother's, mother's, mother's father."

"Oh boy. What's his name?"

"His name is OPA."

"What does OPA mean?"

"OPA means grandfather."

Ian blurted out "So, he was my great-great-OPA!"

"That's right, Ian."

"Did you know him, Grandfather?"

"I sure did."

"Did OPA live here with you?"

"No. He lived in Holland."

"So why is he wearing a cowboy hat?"

My wife came over to us and asked: "What are you two up to?"

Ian answered, "I was trying to figure out why my great-great-OPA was wearing a cowboy hat. Grandfather said you would like to tell me the story."

"Well, about thirty years ago, OPA, who was my grandfather, came from Holland to visit us here in Rochester all by himself. It was the first time that OPA had flown in a plane, his first journey outside of Holland, and his first visit to America. He was ninety years old!"

"Was he scared?"

"No. In fact, while he was staying with us, he made another plane trip to Canada. "He went to visit one of his seven sons, whom he had not seen in ten years. It was at the time of the rodeo in Calgary, Alberta."

"Did his son buy the cowboy hat for OPA?"

"No. But OPA's son introduced him to the mayor of Calgary and told him all about OPA's age and his travels alone. The mayor was impressed. So, he presented OPA with the keys to the city, and crowned him with a cowboy hat."

"Like a cowboy king!" Ian added.

"Yes, he was a king." his grandmother agreed.

"And who is this little girl holding OPA's hand?"

"That's your own mother. You look like her."

Ian studied the picture for the longest time.

"My mom? Naaaaw. No way. I don't believe that's her. She's too small."

My wife and I laughed at that and explained.

"Your mom was only eight years old when the picture was taken. The same age as you are now."

No More Macaroni

Wish I wasn't twelve years old. Can't wait to grow up. Get away from this house, run away from this place, run away from it all. People telling me what to do, what not to do. My little brother always asking dumb questions, wanting to play baby games. Drops his toys all over the house. Nearly broke my toe on his truck last night. Never leaves my stuff alone. Nothing's safe with him around. Guess he's all right though, just a kid.

Dad's always traveling, working, tired when he gets home. Doesn't notice me much. Talks to me a few minutes, then has other things to do. Make phone calls, write letters, and work on his papers. Locks himself up with the computer.

When Dad and I play games, he always says the same old things. "Come on, Dan, try harder. Play to win! Got to win you know. Don't want to be a loser, do you boy?" But when I win, he gets mad and walks off.

Dad and Mom shout at each other. Can hear them at night through my bedroom wall. Money, money, money! Don't understand why they fight so much. Scares me. Makes me nervous. Have to hide my head under the pillow. Try not to hear them. Try to sleep.

This morning, Dad went away again on one of his trips. Won't be back for a week. It's nice and quiet when he goes away. But then I miss him and wish he was here. And sometimes I hope he would never come back.

Love my mom. Love it when she hugs me. Always smells so nice. I try to do what she says, but I can't all the time. It's hard on Mom to look after four kids. All by herself most of the time. Wish she didn't have to go to work. Gets home late some evenings. We hardly ever eat decent meals. Spaghetti, macaroni, spaghetti, macaroni; out of a can.

Mom and Dad absent a lot, so I am free to do what I want. Hang around with the gang. Play lots of games. Can't stand it when they win. Makes me mad. Makes me feel like nothing, like a crumb. Always trying harder and harder.

The kids tease me about my clothes. Have to wear my older brother's hand-me-downs. Never fit, look crummy. They say I'm a loser. But I'll show them.

School is okay. Biology is real cool, cutting up the animals, seeing all their parts. Some kids can't touch them, think they are gross. Sorry for those kids, sorry for the animals. Love math and science. Straight A's. That'll show them. I'm gonna be a doctor. My mom and dad will be proud of me.

Hate to come home from school. Mom won't be here. My sister and her girl-friends will be watching TV. Nibbling on chips. Raiding the fridge. Wonder why they giggle when they see me? Whispering and giggling.

My room is the greatest place. Get a chance to be alone. Nobody to pester me. Can sit and think of all the things I'd like to do. Read about all the places I'll travel to when I grow up.

I hear the door. Mom's home. Better help her with the groceries. Will we have a real dinner tonight? Oh for some beef! Roast beef and mashed potatoes with apple pie and ice cream for dessert. What I would give for a good, thick, juicy hamburger. Please Mom, no more macaroni.

DANNIE'S GAME

The ping-pong table was set up in the garage. Four boys milled around outside, waiting for a turn to play. Dan stayed inside to watch the game, getting ready to take on the winner. He sat on the edge of an old metal chair, biting his nails, knocking his knees together in rhythm with the bouncing ball. Suddenly, Dan jumped up and sent the chair flying backwards. He paced in small circles, cracked his knuckles, rubbed his hands together, clenched and unclenched his fists. His lips moved, but no sounds came out.

Tight Bermuda shorts hugged his narrow, twelve-year-old hips, and the white T-shirt looked too small. Dan must have had to wriggle into his clothes. He bent down and carefully pulled up the thin socks that had slid down over dirty sneakers; at that moment, the game was over. "Big Gary" had won and called out, "Hey, Dannie boy, your turn! Got to play me again. Get your skinny little body over here."

Dan grabbed the paddle from the loser's hand and took his place. Apprehension showed in his eyes because Gary was a tough opponent.

Dan lost the first five points on his own serve and shook his head in disbelief. The score reached 10/5, and he was still losing, despite all efforts to lunge, leap, spring, and stretch. Strain began to show; neck muscles were rigid, face flushed pink, as Dan constantly wiped away sweat with quick, short movements.

With the score at 17/13 against him, Dan was desperate. The other boys gathered to watch the last part of the game. Dan glanced furtively at them and commented loudly when he or Gary made an error.

"Stupid idiot. I can't do anything right today."

"Think you're great, eh Gary? The game's not over yet."

"Got you that time, lousy serve."

"Couldn't return my smash. Too hot for you, Gary!"

Dan's game fell apart; he was out of control, then it was all over. At 21/17, Gary raised his paddle in a taunting victory salute.

Dan flew into a rage, banged the table with the paddle, threw it on the floor, stamped on the little plastic ball, and shouted: "Won again this time, you jerk. But I'm better than you. Let's play again, and I'll show you."

Gary, still smirking, replied, "Dan, you twerp, know what? You're a poor loser, the world's worst. Always were, always will be."

This humiliated Dan in front of his friends and made him angrier. He raced around the table and started scuffling with Gary. With one deft move, Gary threw Dan and pinned him to the concrete floor so that he could not move.

"Surrender, Dan?"

"Yes. I surrender," he conceded, and Gary released him. Dan stayed on his back for a few moments, rigid as a board, then sprang up, pulled up his socks, turned away from the group, and fled from the garage, eyes focused on the ground.

He started to cry. His body was trembling, and tears streamed down his face; he pressed both hands around his head as if to prevent it from falling off. Words came jerkily between sobs. "Dunce. Featherbrain. Bonehead. Nerd. I made so many mistakes. Could have won, beaten him. Just wait until next time!"

ROSES FOR AUDREY
AN INTERVIEW WITH AUDREY HEPBURN

She walked over to me, put her hand on my shoulder, and said, "Ron, I'm all yours now."

That was Audrey Hepburn, saying she was ready for the interview she had promised me a few days earlier.

We were in our home on Longboat Key, Florida. She loved to visit the key for its pristine beauty, to admire the birds, to walk bare-foot on the sand, and to enjoy the congeniality of the area.

It was an unusually cool mid-morning in November. Audrey was dressed casually and looked neat in a blue sweatshirt and slacks, her dark brown hair tied back in a little bun on the back of her neck. I told her that I had chosen a single subject for the interview—roses.

I knew that Audrey had traveled all over the world for personal reasons and as an ambassador for UNICEF.

Also, she had recently undertaken a project to visit some of the world's most beautiful gardens. This project culminated in a television series for PBS called "Gardens of the World with Audrey Hepburn" and a book titled *Gardens of the World.*"

I asked her what was the most beautiful rose garden she had ever seen. She answered without hesitating.

"One of the most beautiful is at Mottisfont Abbey in England, started by Graham Thomas," she said. "It is one of the best collections of old roses in the world."

We chatted about that particular garden for a while, then I pressed on, asking her to name her three favorite roses. She responded immediately, and without any prompting from me, proceeded to give some of the reasons for her choices.

First, she mentioned the Alliance rose because the blooms open totally to display their hearts and purest white petals. Then the Grand Siecle, a large, barely pink rose that is highly scented. Finally Queen Elizabeth, a floribunda with strong, shiny, green leaves and generous blooms from June to November.

I was anxious to discover her reaction to the fact that a dramatic new rose had just been named for her. I showed her a photograph I had brought along of the Audrey Hepburn rose, and asked her how she felt about this apple-blossom pink beauty.

Her eyes and face lit up as if she were playing a scene from *"Breakfast at Tiffany's."*

"Ron, it is the most romantic thing that could ever happen to you," she beamed.

"Were there any other flowers named after you?" I asked.

"A white tulip," she replied.

"What was it called?" I asked, realizing right away that it was a silly question.

"Well, you know..." and she paused

"The Audrey Hepburn tulip," I added.

She smiled, and we understood that out of genuine modesty she had not wanted to say it herself. At this point, she interjected that her favorites are white flowers.

Audrey was genuinely happy and thoughtful in responding to my questions. Her answers came briskly in her usual alert and self-confident manner, reflecting the fact that she had a keen interest and wide knowledge about roses in particular and gardening in general.

I had once seen her garden in Switzerland.

"How many rose bushes are there in your garden?" I asked.

"Oh, about 500," she replied, "with about 20 different kinds of roses, some just for cutting and others for more lasting beauty outside in the garden."

A gardener looked after spraying and general maintenance of the roses, but Audrey liked to disbud some to produce single, perfect, large blooms, and also enjoyed cutting off old, faded roses to maintain the vigor of the plants. I had promised that it would be a short interview, so I brought it to a close by asking and age-old question

"Why do you think God made rose bushes so full of thorns?"

She did not take long to reply. "They are so beautiful that they need to defend themselves. Also remember, Ron, people can be prickly, too, but we don't reject or discard them for having prickles."

I started out to talk with Audrey about roses, and came away thinking about modesty, beauty, caring, generosity, and human understanding.

I also understood why so many people all over the world admired and loved her, and liked to send roses to this Fair Lady.

Postscript: Audrey Hepburn died on January 20, 1993. There are always roses on her grave in Tolochenaz, Switzerland.

SHAGGY THE RASTAMAN
THE MEANING OF I.R.I.E.

The four letters I.R.I.E stood out in red on the black man's yellow T-shirt. I was intrigued by the fact that they were scrawled in so many places throughout the island. Was I R I E a word or an abbreviation? What did it mean?

The man was an imposing figure as he waited on the sidewalk, his face framed by long braids of matted hair known as dreadlocks. A taxi stopped in front of him. A well-dressed white woman with straight, flowing, black hair stepped out, cuddling two babies in her arms. My wife and I hurried over to admire the babies, also using that as an excuse to start a conversation.

Her name was Maria; her husband's name was Shaggy. Mr. and Mrs. Shaggy Dread were in their mid-twenties.

"Are your babies twins?" I asked.

"Yes," he replied.

"How old are they?"

"Four months."

Maria spoke very little English. She had arrived in Jamaica from Milan, Italy, only two years before. She left us alone with Shaggy, walked down a lane, and disappeared into a small house.

Shaggy is a Rastafarian. This sect believes in the divinity of the man named *Ras Tafari,* who was crowned Haile Selassie, Emperor of Ethiopia in the year 1930.

Anxious to explore their doctrine, I asked:

"Shaggy, do you personally believe that Haile Selassie is God?"

"Well, yes. I don't call upon a God who I can't see. Dat's impossible. God is not a spirit. A God mus' talk, an' walk, an' drink, an' eat Uncle Ben's rice."

"How did you come to believe that, Shaggy?"

"Well, since I was a young bwoy, I had dat strong concep'. 'E is de Messiah, de King of Kings, de Lord of Lords, comin' from de tribe of David. 'E is the Livin' God."

"But do you realize that Haile Selassie is dead?"

"All people die many times y'u know."

"Were you always Rasta?"

"Yes. Me modder and fahder and brodder was Rasta. The King is Ras Tafari, and I is Ras Tafari."

"Are there different types of Rastamen?"

"Yes. Dere is t'ree kinds. Firs' is a culture man like I, who can sing, an' argue, an' discuss. Den some dat jus' grow long hair to go around an' hustle people, an' sleep wid dem American girls on de beach fo' money. Den t'ird there is de Binjie man who live up in the mountain, grow food, meditate, smoke grass, and love all de people."

Shaggy was a friendly, aggressive, and forthright man. He spoke in a proud, assertive, and confident manner. In fact, the Rastas have constructed a language of their own. In regular Jamaican Creole language, the first person singular pronoun "I" is expressed as "me", as in "Me have money" and "Me eat banana." But Rastafarians consider the word "me" subservient and self-degrading; in contrast, they believe the word "I", and the plural "I-and-I" (for "we"), identifies them as individuals. They might even add the letter "I" to the beginning or end of a word, as in the names of Shaggy's children, Naka-I and Hali-I.

Shaggy was starting to look restless, so I finally asked the big question. "By the way, Shaggy, what's the meaning of I. R. I. E. on your T-shirt?"

Throwing back his shaggy head and pointing to his chest, he replied with obvious pride. "I R I E means I RASTA I ETHIOPIAN."

And so the puzzle was solved. Shaggy shook hands with I, and then I-and-I parted as if I-and-I were old friends.

Ronald E. Glegg

POLLENATION

Oriental lilies wear their high-fashion dresses
When they dance their delicate tangos in my garden.
Some turn their faces up to the sun
Seeking praise from some place far away.
Others bend their hatted heads
And look toward the ground
Too humble, too shy to be seen in all their finery.
Their perfumes match the colors of their skins
So soft, so fragile, not to be touched just seen.
Bees, butterflies, and hummingbirds come around
To taste the nectar.
Drunk with excitement, mad with desire
They fly away, silent as they go
After kissing the fragrant dancing ladies.

LOVE AND TICKLES

Strolling through a park one summer afternoon
I bent down to collect some pinecones underneath a tree.
What do you think I spied between some leaves?
A little elf! About the size of a honey bee—
And fast asleep!
I gently picked him up and took him home with me.
On close inspection, the imp was holding a bow and arrow.
Who do you think he turned out to be?
The little traitor,--cupid!
We lived happily together. But one evening, while playing,
He jumped into my third glass of wine.
In one quick gulp
I accidentally swallowed him.
I was sure I had killed cupid and wondered
If I had put and end to love forever.
But guess what?
At this very moment, I can feel the little trickster
Tickling my heartstrings.
Cupid is alive, well and happy!

ON A SUMMER AFTERNOON

Touching down with soft, silent glide
Painted paper wings unfold in unison,
Revealing patterns of refined tattoos,
That imitates the hues of orchids.
Brief flutterings, fleeting metamorphosis,
Too short a span for deep experiences.
Born to flit away, dissolve like clouds,
Essence of mortality.
Standing watch as at a wake
The flowers share their nectar,
Whisper farewell and mourn with me
The passage of a butterfly.

NO FOREVERS

Rub the past like a sacred stone
Discover blessings of childhood year
Spilling over from yesterdays.
Anticipation of joyful images
Blue mountains, scarlet twilights,
Mustard yellow beaches, cornmeal sand,
Green banana trees in perfect rows.
Memories of prized experiences
Birthdays, exchanging kisses,
Waiting for a fish to bite,
Ice cream melting in the sun,
Hide-and-seek, growing up.
Disappointment-shock.
Neglected kids, starved, abused by nature,
Shoeless, flies on their eyes,
Orphaned, homeless.
Sick people limping, sightless.
Everyone aging, senility.
Dead people, dead friends,
Young birds rotting on the grass.
Graves of mother and father

Ronald E. Glegg

Stifling fragrance of sympathetic flowers,
Litany of grief, death, sadness
Then going back home after Christmas,
To cold, lonely New Year's Eve.

RUM

Rum runs like antelopes
In unison with drunken dreams
Of smoke and sexuality.
As if to run amuck
In devastation
It lasts 'til time runs out.
Sodden and satiated
It finds its way to the underworld
Cloaked in the niceties of society.
Amusing sire of indiscretion and relief
It gently rocks the drunken fools to sleep.

SUNSET AT PASS-A-GRILLE

The historic town of Pass-A-Grille slumbers on a narrow tongue of land where Boca Ciega Bay kisses the Gulf of Mexico on the southern tip of Saint Petersburg Beach in Florida. Soon, the sun will set across the gulf. From my balcony overlooking the water, I can watch it unobstructed. I become aware of the sounds of waves and changing hues of clouds. Hundreds of glistening coquina clams bore into the wet, white sand, and birds are everywhere.

Sunset lovers saunter down to the beach, drawn by the magic of late afternoon. Some sit as if in church with reverence for the glorious occasion about to unfold; others take up a special stance as if preparing to assist.

Birds enjoy sunsets, too. A pelican flies best just before the sun goes down, showing off for the last time that day. Silhouetted against the sky, its graceful glide suddenly transforms into a vertical dive aimed at the center of the earth. The wings fold tightly; the beak, head, neck, and body shoot straight down like a black arrow into the water. A surprised fish pushes water through its gills for the last time before it slips into the swollen pouch below the neck of the hungry bird. The pelican takes off from the water, desperately flapping feet and waterproof wings, revving its motor to leave the runway.

Sandpipers scurry across the sand, spindly legs moving at incredible speed for such small birds. They gather in groups of thirty or more, and move in unison, like soldiers marching in formation.

I concentrate on the setting sun, and when the strongest rays are diluted by its proximity to the horizon, I admire the red, round ball. The sun sinks faster as it finally decides to hide and cool itself in the sea. The indigo line of the horizon slices into the sun, diminishing it, until the last precious piece of the orb disappears. People smile, laugh, and applaud, then drift away. The colors, sights, and sounds remind me to be happy, peaceful, and grateful to be alive.

I think of the many people who have turned to the west, witnessed the sun setting, and guided it down. In awe of the experience, in being one with nature and the universe, I linger to think about the mystery and anticipate the light and the warmth of the next day, and the next.

THE TEA MIND
(CHADO, THE WAY OF TEA)

The words of the Japanese poet Kyoshi set the mood as we joined ten other guests to witness a tea ceremony:

> When the autumn wind
> Blows there is but poetry
> In all things I find.

Japanese Zen Buddhism developed the spirit of *Chado*, the philosophy of tea, the way of Tea. It embodies the four principles of harmony, respect, purity, and tranquility.

A basic part of Zen experience is that man and nature must live in harmony. The concept is a driving force behind the present need to resolve our ecological problems, like the preservation of rain forests, ozone depletion, and survival of the spotted owl.Respect entails a genuine appreciation of our fellow human beings, recognizing their dignity, and seeing the merits in the lives of people of all walks of life. Respect requires empathy, and is the guiding principle for the enlightened practice of acceptable human relations.

Purity dictates that the body, heart, and mind should be clean and orderly. This leads to the idea that the same forces of technology that contribute to pollution of our environment are responsible for polluting our human circumstances.

Tranquility is achieved by practicing these three principles: harmony, respect, and purity. It is a spiritual state leading to the discovery of one's own nature and innermost being; it divorces us from the worries and stresses of the world.

The four principles are reflected in many aspects of the teahouse and the tea ceremony. The teahouse and its contents display the beauty to be found and admired in simple, natural materials. The architecture is that of a peasant's hut, constructed of bare, unpainted wood. There are no chairs or stools; the floor is covered with straw mats known as tatamis. The host and guest are equal as they kneel opposite one another; they interact without speaking aloud, but communicate with body language made up of smiles and bows, by their mutual admiration of the place and one another, and by reading each other's mind, known as the "tea mind."

The folding fan held by the guest is a symbol of respect and goodwill. Several of the utensils are made of bamboo, which represents flexibility and resilience. As an act of humility, the host prepares green tea while the guest looks on, instead of the tea being prepared out of sight and brought by servants.

Water is boiled, green powered tea is measured out and placed in a ceramic bowl with the water, and then the mixture is stirred to a frothy consistency with a bamboo whisk. The design on the tea bowl is a work of art to be inspected, studied, and admired by the guest in whose hand it is placed by the host. The tea is bitter and unsweetened.

The ceremony begins with the pouring of cool water in a symbolic act of purity. The bowl is wiped by the host with a red cloth in a ritual, which coupled with the small, slightly sweet rice cakes offered as an accompaniment, is reminiscent of the celebration of communion in a Roman Catholic church. In a sense, the tea ceremony is a religious experience.

The atmosphere surrounding the ceremony was honest, frugal, and unpretentious, and it was conducive to feelings of compassion, understanding, tranquility, purity, respect, and harmony. A single bowl of tea shared by host and guest, the Way of Tea, might well serve as a model for easing the divisions of personal animosities, racial tension, and international discord.